## Mark's dilemma was as strong as ever

There was something about Emily's spark, her spirit, that made him feel more alive than he had in months. But he couldn't ignore the other part, either—the part that wanted to protect his son's heart by keeping her at arm's length.

"Don't get close, don't get hurt," he mumbled under his breath.

It was a good motto. One that would keep him from ever seeing the kind of heart-wrenching hurt he'd been unable to erase from Seth's eyes during Sally's illness.

*Emily.*

Once again, the woman who'd captivated his son over a sand castle and a pepperoni pizza flashed before his eyes.

Emily was struggling on the first rung of a ladder he knew all too well. He saw it in her face when he talked to her about the foundation. He heard it in her voice when she brushed off his concern about the pain in her leg. And he sensed it in the unbendable determination that made her refuse help for even the simplest of things.

She needed a hand.

Dear Reader,

I've written my fair share of books over the past several years, but none have impacted me in quite the way this one has.

Like my heroine, Emily Todd, I, too, was diagnosed with Multiple Sclerosis. And like Emily, I found myself doubting who I was and what I'd be able to do with my life.

Fortunately for me, I have a lot of the same drive Emily has, and I soon realized that those big scary words didn't have to change much of anything. And they haven't. I still do everything I've always done and you'd be hard-pressed to know there's anything wrong with me.

While the rest of my story is very different than Emily's, both of us experienced the unconditional love of a child along our path to acceptance. For Emily, that child is Mark's son, Seth. For me, it was my then-eight-year-old daughter, whose love and steadfast hand helped me turn a necessary corner in the way I saw things.

Life certainly comes with its fair share of surprises, doesn't it? Thankfully, love has a way of making most of those surprises work out just fine.

With warm hugs,

Laura Bradford

# Storybook Dad
## LAURA BRADFORD

**HARLEQUIN**®
entertain, enrich, inspire™

Recycling programs
for this product may
not exist in your area.

ISBN-13: 978-0-373-75428-1

STORYBOOK DAD

**Printed in U.S.A.**

## ABOUT THE AUTHOR

Since the age of ten, Laura Bradford hasn't wanted to do anything other than write—news articles, feature stories, business copy and whatever else she could come up with to pay the bills. But they were always diversions from the one thing she wanted to write most—fiction.

Today, with an Agatha Award nomination under her belt and a new mystery series with Berkley Prime Crime, Laura is thrilled to have crossed into the romance genre with her all-time favorite series, Harlequin American Romance.

When she's not writing, Laura enjoys reading, hiking, traveling and all things chocolate. She lives in New York with her two daughters. To contact her, visit her website, www.laurabradford.com.

### Books by Laura Bradford
#### HARLEQUIN AMERICAN ROMANCE

For Jenny,

You were, without a doubt, Mommy's biggest hero
during a very difficult time.
You are an amazingly special little girl
and I'm blessed to be able to call you my daughter.

## Chapter One

Emily Todd stared down at the sparkly silver castle and the blue-eyed prince standing in front of its door, a familiar lump rising in her throat. Oh, what she wouldn't give to rewind time back to when planning life's path had been as easy as reaching for the next crayon in a brand-new sixty-four-count pack.

Back then, with the help of Giddy-Up Brown, she'd been able to ride the perfect horse through a canopy of Burnt Autumn leaves. A mixture of River Brown and Nautical Gray had captured the hue of an angry river with the indisputable eye of a future rafter, while Foliage Green had breathed life into the woods she'd navigated with a slightly oversized compass. And Rocky Ledge? The curious mixture of brown, blue and gray? That had made the mountain she'd squeezed onto its own piece of eighteen-by-twenty-four-inch manila paper seem both majestic and ominous at the same time.

It was hard not to look at the framed pictures on the wall behind her desk and not be impressed by the colors her pint-sized self had selected when mapping out her life in crayon. Though why she hadn't grown bored with the whole notion of drawing her dreams after the fourth picture was anyone's guess—even if Milk Chocolate Brown hair and Ocean Wave Blue eyes were still her ideal for the prince who'd never materialized.

Shaking her head, Emily slipped the decades-old castle drawing back into the folder and pushed it across the desk at her best friend. "Look, I know what you're trying to do here, Kate, but this doesn't mean anything to me anymore. It's a drawing. A silly, stupid drawing. I mean, really, what guy carries a woman across a threshold these days unless she's an invalid and can't make it through the door herself?"

She considered her own words, compared them to the nightmare that had driven her out of bed before dawn, the same one that had robbed her of sleep many times over the past few weeks. "Hmm. Now that I think about it, I should have spent my Saturday afternoons running a fortune-telling operation instead of all those lemonade stands we used to have as kids, huh? I think I actually had a visionary gift."

Ignoring the blatant sarcasm in Emily's voice, Kate Jennings pointed at the series of framed pictures behind Emily's head. "You framed *those* drawings, didn't you? So what's the difference?"

She glanced over her shoulder, mentally comparing herself to the girl in each of the four drawings. Her hair, while still the same natural blond it had always been, was now fashioned in a pixie cut in lieu of the long locks she'd preferred as a child. Her big brown eyes hadn't changed at all, really, only they didn't sparkle quite as much. And the faint smattering of freckles noticeably absent in the drawings was right where it had always been, sprinkled across the bridge of her nose like fairy dust. "I can think of one huge difference, Kate. The dreams depicted in the frames? Those actually came true. That one—" she pointed at the folder "—didn't."

Kate pushed the folder back toward Emily. "So what? You drew them all at the same time."

She felt the tension building in her shoulders and worked to keep it from her voice. "Do you think a doctor would frame a term paper she'd failed, and hang it in her office beside her medical school diploma? Do you think an architect would want to showcase her first ever set of plans—the ones where she forgot to add the foundation that would have actually kept the structure *standing?*" At Kate's scowl, Emily continued. "I think it's cool that you found these pictures after all this time, Kate, I really do. It's why I framed the four I did. But you can't expect me to be too eager to glorify an unrealized dream alongside ones that actually came true, can you?"

Without waiting for a response, Emily pushed back her desk chair and stood. "I've got to get back to work. I have an orienteering class starting in five minutes." She strode across the office, stopping at the door. "But I'll see you and Doug on Friday night at the barbecue, right?"

"Definitely." Kate grabbed the folder and her purse and met Emily at the door. "It's not supposed to be too hot that day, so you should be—"

"I'll be fine no matter what the temperature is," she snapped. Then, realizing how she sounded, she softened her tone. "This diagnosis is not going to beat me, Kate. You of all people should know that. I've done everything I said I was going to do and then some."

"If that were true, this picture—" Kate waved the folder in the air "—would be in a frame like all the others."

"Would you give it a rest, please? I'm not going to hang my failures on the wall. Seems kind of morbid to me."

"I get that," Kate said, tucking the folder under her arm. "But the horseback riding, the kayaking—all of it—came true because you set your mind to it and you made it happen. I mean, c'mon, Emily, how many people do we know from our childhood who have started their own company? How many people do we know that have taken said company and made it the talk of, not only this town, but every other town in a hundred-mile radius? None that I can think of. And why is that? Because you made up your mind about what you wanted in life a very long time ago. So why should finding Mr. Wonderful be any different now?"

"Because *I'm* different now," she whispered.

Kate reached out and brushed a wisp of hair from her friend's face. "Did you ever consider the possibility that all this other stuff came true first because you were *able* to do it at that time?"

Emily closed her eyes, the familiar pull of fear that had accompanied the doctor's diagnosis threatening to envelop her all over again.

No. She refused to go there again. Not now, anyway. Not when she had a class to teach.

Opening her eyes, she gave Kate a hug and then shoved her through the door, her voice settling somewhere between frustration and determination. "I was and *am* able to do it, Kate. Nothing is going to change that. You just wait and see."

"But if you'd just slow down long enough to meet someone, you might—"

"Please. I've got to go. I'll see you Friday evening."

Without waiting for a response, Emily made her way toward the classroom at the end of the hall. Her friend was wrong. Scenes in the pictures on the wall had come true because they were up to *Emily*. The Prince Charming picture she'd sent back home with Kate was nothing but a childhood fantasy born at a time when she'd been blissfully naive about words like *disability* and *burden*.

She was wiser now.

Squaring her shoulders, she yanked open the door and walked into the room to find five pairs of eyes greeting her arrival with the same determination that had driven her throughout her life. It was a determination she admired and understood. "Welcome to Bucket List 101. My name is Emily Todd, and I'm here to help you realize your dream of learning how to orienteer your way through the woods with nothing more than a compass and some coordinates. As you probably know from the course description that lured you here, we'll spend our first hour in the classroom learning about the compass and how to use it, along with our maps. Then we'll head out into the woods for some fun."

The left side of the conference table held a trio of retired men who were hanging on every word she spoke. To the right sat the mother-daughter team who'd called the day before looking for some memorable bonding time. "It looks like we've got a good group here," Emily said.

"I hope my presence won't change that."

Spinning around, Emily took in the sight of the man standing in the doorway, registration papers in hand, and froze, her heart thudding in her chest.

"My name's Mark Reynolds. Your assistant at the front desk said I could still get in your class if I hurried."

She knew she should say something. But for a moment she was at a complete loss for words.

Mark Reynolds was like no man she'd ever laid eyes on—at least not outside the confines of her imagination. Even then, the flesh-and-blood version was much taller than she'd always envisioned. Either way though, his hair was the epitome of Milk Chocolate Brown and his eyes a perfect match for Ocean Wave Blue....

But it was his arms—the kind capable of sweeping a woman off her feet and carrying her across the threshold of a make-believe castle—that yanked Emily back to a reality that no longer had room for such silly dreams.

Mark looked down at his registration papers and then back at Emily. "So…am I too late?"

Slowly she expelled the breath she hadn't realized she'd been holding. "It's never too late, Mr. Reynolds. Not for *learning,* anyway."

HE HUNG BACK as they neared the parking lot, his thoughts as much on Emily Todd as anything he'd learned that morning. During the first hour of class, before they'd ventured outside, they'd sat around a table, and Emily had taught them how to use a compass to find a set of coordinates. He'd tried to listen politely to the questions his classmates asked, and had worked hard to focus on the answers, but in the end, all he knew for sure was the fact that his teacher was gorgeous.

Emily Todd was straight out of the pages of one of his son's favorite fairy tales, right down to the wispy blond hair, slightly upturned nose and big brown doe eyes. But unlike those winged characters that flew around in the dark, sprinkling pixie dust in the air, this woman's feet were firmly on the ground, and she carried herself with a confidence that was anything but childlike.

He admired the determination that had driven her to start a company like Bucket List 101. It took guts and—judging by the list of outdoor activities the company offered—she had to be in great physical shape. Her toned legs and taut body attested to that.

"Did you enjoy yourself, Mr. Reynolds?"

Mark shifted his attention from Emily to her teenage assistant. "I had a great time, Trish. Spending the last two hours in the woods was really cool."

"It's one of my favorite classes, too." Trish swept her clipboard toward Emily, who was disappearing into the woods with a drawstring bag. "Every time I think Emily has come up with the coolest class ever, she trumps it with another one the next time around. Come January, she'll be offering this same class, but on skis."

"Skis?"

"Sounds awesome, doesn't it?" Without waiting for his answer, Trish headed across the parking lot, glancing back over her shoulder in his direction. "If you're interested, I'll be in the office tomorrow morning. We can get you signed up before the fall and winter program guide even goes out in the mail."

"Thanks, Trish. Sounds like fun." And it did.

Especially since it meant spending more time with Emily Todd...

"Don't you think you should give that back to Emily before you get in your car and drive home?"

Mark pulled his gaze from Emily's receding back and fixed it instead on one of the retired guys, who'd kept the class in stitches with his nonstop jokes throughout the three-hour course. "Huh?"

The man pointed at Mark's left hand. "You still have your compass. You were supposed to set it on the porch railing when we came out of the woods."

"Whoops. You're right. I'd guess I better catch up with Trish and turn this in before Emily thinks I made off with her equipment."

"If I were you, young man, I'd bypass Trish and take it straight to Emily. Gives you an excuse to look at her for another few minutes."

Raking his hand through his hair, Mark released an audible breath. "No, man, it's not like that. Really. I've got a kid at home and I'm not in any place to be—"

"She's a cute little thing. Spunky, too." The man took a few steps and then paused. "And she don't have no wedding ring on her finger, either."

Mark looked down at the hand that gripped the compass, a familiar lump building in his throat at the sight of the half-inch band of skin that no longer stood out the way it once had when his ring was off. What on earth was he doing? He'd taken this class as a release, not to pick up chicks. It was way too soon. Seth needed his complete focus. *He* needed his complete focus....

Mark started back across the grass and along the path where Emily had just disappeared. Step by step, he ventured farther into the woods, and found the excitement he'd felt during the hands-on portion of the class resurfacing in spades.

It was as if the sunlight that randomly poked through the heavy leaves, warming him from the outside in, had somehow managed to rekindle a part of his spirit that had disappeared along with any respect he'd once had for himself prior to Sally's death.

Mark climbed onto a stump and looked from side to side, his heart rate picking up at the sight of Emily heading back toward him, the bag she'd been carrying into the woods now looped over her shoulder, a pad of paper and a pencil in her hand. "Emily? I saw you head back here. Everything okay?"

She stopped midstep and gave him a funny look. "Just jotting down a few new coordinates for next time. Did you forget something, Mr. Reynolds?"

"No, I..." He glanced down, saw the compass he held in a death grip. "Actually, yeah. I forgot to turn in my compass. By the time I realized it, Trish had already collected them and I didn't want to just leave it sitting around."

The smile he'd found so engaging all afternoon returned. "Kind of got used to holding it, huh? Well, don't worry about it. I've found myself driving home with a compass still in my hand after one of these kinds of outings, so you're in good company. Means it started to feel natural."

He tucked the compass into his pants pocket and swept his gaze across the woods, nodding. "I can't believe how good it felt to be out here...playing."

Her laughter echoed around them. "Welcome to my job. Where I get to play—and help others play—all day long."

"Sounds like heaven to me."

"Really? Because the last time *I* checked these woods were in the middle of Winoka, Wisconsin," she joked, before beckoning him to follow as she wound her way back through the trees. "If you don't mind me asking, what made you decide to take this class, Mr. Reynolds?"

He considered the best way to respond. If he shared too much, the lift in his heart from stepping out of his reality would be gone. If he didn't give her any kind of answer, he'd come across as rude. He opted for the safest reply he could find. "First of all, it's Mark. Mr. Reynolds makes me feel as if you're talking to someone much older than I want to be. And as to why I came today, I guess you could say I'm looking for something that'll help me unwind."

"Sounds like a good reason."

They emerged from the woods side by side, then cut across the clearing toward the old converted barn that served as the offices for Bucket List 101. When they reached the front door, Mark tried to think of something else to say, something to allow him even a few more minutes in her orbit, but he came up empty.

"Well, thanks for today. It was really great."

"I'm glad you enjoyed it, Mr. Reynolds."

"Mark," he reminded her gently. At her nod, he turned and headed toward his car, the sound of the door opening and shutting behind him making it both easier and harder to breathe. Never in his recent and not-so-recent memory could he recall a woman who affected him quite the way Emily did.

Except, of course, for Sally. And even then, it was for very different reasons....

When he got to his car he reached into his pocket for his keys and froze.

"Oh, no…" He wrapped his fingers around the circular object and pulled it out, denial quickly morphing into self-recrimination. "What an idiot I am!"

Shaking his head, he retraced his steps to the barn and went inside, his feet guided down the hall by the sound of music and a pinpoint of light streaming through the crack under a door.

He knocked and heard Emily say, "Come in."

Pushing the door open, Mark peeked inside, to find her hunched at a desk, poring over some sort of outdoor catalog. "I'm sorry to bother you, but I forgot to actually *give* you my compass after tracking you down in the woods. I'm a head case, I know."

Her laugh echoed off the walls and brought his body to attention. "Considering the fact that you showed it to me twenty minutes ago and I didn't take it, I think it's safe to say your state of mind isn't the only one in question at the moment. But no worries. I happen to believe momentary insanity is par for the course after running through the woods for two hours the way we did. It rattles brains, I think."

He took a few steps into her office and leaned against the wall, her sincerity and her genuineness speaking to him on some unexpected level. "Do you ever get tired, running around like that?"

The sparkle in her eyes dimmed. "No, never."

"Wow." Despite his best intentions, he found himself glancing around the room, looking for any excuse to stretch out their time together. It was as if by being there, talking to her, he could almost forget the unforgettable. He pointed at the illustrations on the wall behind her desk. "Looks like you've got a budding artist on your hands."

The sparkle returned. "Nope. Just a dreamer who happens to have a very sentimental friend."

"You lost me."

She grinned. "I drew those when I was ten. Kate, my sentimental friend, just uncovered them in her hope chest a few weeks ago, and felt the need to share them."

He took a step toward the pictures. "And this is you in all of these?"

"Minus the freckles, of course. I hated my freckles when I was ten."

"You shouldn't have." He pointed at the first drawing. "Trail riding?"

"That'll start back up in the spring."

Stepping to the right, he considered the second. "Nice rapids in this one."

Her laugh sent a skitter of awareness down his spine. "If I took my customers white-water rafting without helmets today, I'd lose my license."

"Artistic liberties, that's all." He matched her laugh and took in the third picture. "Something tells me I didn't look quite as confident in the woods just now with *my* compass."

"You did great." Emily swiveled her chair a hairbreadth to study him. "Everyone did."

Aware of her gaze, he pointed to the final picture. "I've always wanted to rock climb."

"Then why haven't you?"

He stared at the drawing, his lips forming the words he'd only recently come to acknowledge. "Procrastination, I guess. I figured there'd always be time. "

"And now?"

"I know better." He cleared his throat of its sudden gruffness and gestured toward the line of framed pictures. "Looks to me like the dreamer who drew these hit a grand slam."

Her silence made him turn just in time to see her open her eyes and force another smile to her lips. "Considering my sentimental friend uncovered a fifth, which I opted not to hang, I'll settle for a home run."

"Oh? What happened to *that* dream?"

She waved his question aside. "To borrow your words, Mr. Reynolds—I mean *Mark*—now I know better."

Momentarily unsure of what to say, he shoved his hands into his pockets and reclaimed his spot against the wall opposite her desk. "Well, four out of five is nothing to sneeze at. Hell, when I was ten, all I thought about was being a firefighter and trying to kiss the redhead who sat behind me in math."

"And how'd you do?"

"One for two."

She laughed. "You're a firefighter, then?"

"No. An accountant."

"So the redhead inspired your academic path?"

"She inspired me to quit putting off until tomorrow."

"Oh?" Emily's eyebrows rose. "Does she need a job? We could use a spokesperson."

"No. No, she doesn't need a job." With his good mood rapidly spiraling, Mark tipped his head forward and pushed himself from the wall. "I'd better get out of here. Lunch-making duties await." He took two steps toward the door and stopped, a flash of color out of the corner of his eye hijacking his attention to the floor. "Oh…hey, you dropped something."

Squatting down, he retrieved a tattered pamphlet from the carpet beside the trash can and turned it over in his hands, the headline, Multiple Sclerosis, catching him by surprise. "You know someone with MS?"

When she didn't answer, he reached into his back pocket and pulled out a business card. "I volunteer with an organization called Folks Helping Folks. We help people with disabilities by building wheelchair ramps, installing handrails in bathrooms, funding specially equipped automobiles, and that sort of thing. You know, whatever can make their day-to-day life a little easier."

Placing the card on top of the pamphlet, he held them out to Emily. When she didn't respond, he held them out farther. Again, she didn't take them, her hands remaining on top of her desk as if glued to its surface. And in that instant he understood why she sat there and said nothing, why she looked at the pamphlet and business card as if they were poison capable of seeping through her skin and into her soul.

He understood because he'd been where she was. He'd loved someone who was sick, too. He knew the fear. He knew the sense of denial that came on the heels of such a bitter experience. And he knew the gut-wrenching pain that came with pulling back.

Leaning across her desk, he set the paperwork in front of her, his heart aching for this beautiful woman who'd allowed him to shed his well-worn cloak of regret and live in the moment for three glorious hours. "I understand where you're at, Emily. I really do. But please, take this anyway. Pass it on to whoever it is you know that's sick. By denying what's going on, all you're doing is hurting yourself and your loved one. Trust me on this."

Then, without realizing what he was doing, he gave her shoulder a gentle squeeze, the warmth of her skin beneath his hand lingering in his thoughts long after Bucket List 101 had faded from his rearview mirror.

# Chapter Two

Tossing her paddle to the shore, Emily maneuvered her way out of the kayak and tugged it onto the sand, the satisfying soreness in her upper arms a welcome relief. No matter how hard she'd tried to bury herself in work the rest of the day, the images spawned by Mark's words had risen to the surface again and again, gnawing at her convictions like a beaver hell-bent on toppling a tree. She'd resisted, of course, but the doubts had claimed a foothold, reappearing throughout the remainder of her workday.

When she'd been teaching her introduction to rock climbing course, she tried to imagine dangling over the side of a cliff in a wheelchair.

When she'd taken a call inquiring about an upcoming white-water rafting trip, she envisioned herself piercing the raft with the end of a cane.

And when she'd locked up her office for the evening and actually considered the notion of wallowing in pity from the confines of her bed, she knew she had to do something. Fast.

Now, two hours later, she felt like herself again. Ready to conquer anything and everything that crossed her path.

Raising her arms in the air, she stretched, the faintest hint of a smile tugging at her lips as she spotted the pint-size towhead feverishly digging in the sand some thirty feet from where she stood. Curious, she closed the gap between them to take a closer look at what the child was doing.

"That's a really nifty castle you're building," she said.

The little boy's hand stilled long enough for him to look up and smile, the deep, penetrating blue of his eyes bringing a momentary hitch to her breath. "Thanks, lady."

She forced her attention back to the castle. "I like all those turrets you built onto the corners."

His cheeks lifted farther as he dropped his shovel in favor of directing Emily's attention toward the tower on the back left corner of his creation. "See that one? That's the princess's room. She's real nice. And this one here—" he shifted his finger to the right "—that's where my room would be if I lived there, too."

Dropping onto the sand beside the boy, Emily retrieved a stick from the ground and secured a nearby leaf to the top. When she was done, she spun it between her fingers while he eyed her across the top of his sand pail. "When I was little, I used to dream about living in a castle, too," she told him. "Only instead of a princess, mine had a handsome prince who would sweep me off my feet every morning and carry me around the castle all day long."

At the child's giggle, she, too, cracked a smile. "That sounds funny," he said.

"Now it does, but when I was young, I thought it sounded romantic." Shaking her head free of the images that threatened to ruin the innocence of the moment, she poked her makeshift flag into the sand by her feet and scrunched up her face. "But don't worry, I don't intend to be carried around by anyone. Ever."

The little boy rocked back on his heels, then jutted his chin in the direction of her stick creation. "That sure would look nice on my castle, don't you think?"

She plucked it from the sand and handed it to him, the answering sparkle in his eyes warming her from head to toe. "But just because my dream was silly doesn't mean you can't share a castle with your princess one day. In fact, I hope you do. Dreams that come true are mighty special."

When he'd positioned the flag just the way he wanted it, the child nodded. "I found an old tree house in the woods behind Gam's house. I like to climb up the ladder all by myself and dream with my eyes open. That way they don't get scary like the ones in my bed."

She studied him for a moment, guessing him to be about four. Maybe just turned five. Either way, he was too young to be alone on the beach....

"What do you dream about in your tree house?" she asked, before squinting down the shoreline.

"Smiles. Lots and lots of smiles."

Startled, she brought her full attention back to the little boy. "Smiles?"

He nodded. "Happy ones. Like the ones me and Daddy used to smile before my mom got sick and went up to heaven."

Emily cast about for something to say, but he didn't give her much of a chance.

"I want us to make great big smiles like that again one day."

"That sounds like a special thing to dream about," she whispered.

"It is." Jumping to his feet, the child surveyed his castle, deeming it a success with a clap of his small hands. "Wow! This is my very bestest castle ever!"

She swung her focus out toward the water and noted the absence of any swimmers or fellow boaters in their immediate vicinity. "You seem awfully little to be out here by yourself."

"I'm not by myself. I'm with my dad." Shooting a pudgy index finger over Emily's shoulder, he pointed toward a man fishing from a line of rocks that led into the lake some twenty or so yards away. "See? He's right there. Fishing."

Shielding the last of the sun's rays from her eyes, she strained to make out the outline standing on the rocks—the tall stature, the broad shoulders, the gray T-shirt and black shorts, the brown hair…

*No. It couldn't be.*

She looked back at the boy. "That man over there is your dad?"

"Yupper doodle." He dropped to a squat and stuck his finger in the sand. Then, slowly but surely, he drew a snake that nearly reached her toes. "My daddy is so smart he taught me how to make my name. See?"

Stepping back, she looked again at the wiggly line and recognized it as an *S*. Three additional letters later, he was done. "Your name is Seth?"

"Yupper doodle." His broad smile reached his bright blue eyes.

*His Ocean Wave Blue eyes…*

She glanced from Seth to the man and back again, the confirmation she sought virtually certain. But still, she asked, "Do you know your last name, Seth?"

"Of course I do, silly. But I can't write that name yet. It's too big and kinda tricky. Especially the first letter." Seth cupped his left hand to the side of his mouth and tipped his head upward. "Gam says I just need to pretend the circle at the top changed its mind and is runnin' away from the line."

Squatting down beside the boy, she left a space between Seth's efforts and her own, talking him through the letter he'd just described. When she was done, she nudged her chin in its direction. "Is this the letter?"

"Yupper doodle." He leaped to his feet and came to stand on the opposite side of Emily. "*R* for R-R-R-Reynolds!"

MARK CRANKED THE REEL slowly, hoping the slight movement would be enough to capture the attention of even one member of the fish population that inhabited Lake Winoka. If it did, at least he'd have something else to think about besides Emily Todd.

From the moment he'd left Bucket List 101, his thoughts had continuously returned to the attractive woman, earning him more than a few curious looks from Seth throughout the afternoon. Mark understood the fear she felt, sympathized with her need to pretend her loved one wasn't ill. He'd been there and done that throughout the entire year leading up to Sally's death.

It had been a mistake. A mistake he'd undo in a heartbeat if given the chance.

But there would be no more chances. He couldn't rewind time no matter how much he wished he could. Instead, he had to find a way to live with the guilt of choosing his job over his dying wife over and over again. At the time it had made such sense. Work was how he coped. The more he worked, the less time he had to think, and to feel.

But it had been wrong. For Sally. For Seth. And for him.

No. Mark wasn't going to let Emily make the same mistakes. Somehow, some way, he was going to help her realize that by facing her loved one's illness head-on, she'd be saving herself the added torture of guilt at the end.

Determined to help, he reeled in the rest of his line and made his way across the rocks. Once he had Seth settled in bed for the night, he could go about putting together a packet of information for Emily. Maybe with more information, she wouldn't feel the need for denial.

And maybe, just maybe, helping Emily would enable him to shed some of his own insomnia-inducing guilt.

He stepped off the last rock and onto the sand and looked toward the castle he'd left Seth to finish while he fished. But instead of finding his son elbow-deep in sand, he spotted him standing beside a kayak and a petite blonde woman.

Mark quickened his pace, only to slow it again as the identity of the women became clear.

"Emily? Is that you?"

"Hi, Mark," she answered.

Eagerly, he jogged forward, fishing pole in hand. "Can I help you get in your kayak?"

A look of something resembling irritation flashed across her face. "If I can lift a kayak on and off my car, and carry it from the parking lot to the lake all by myself, I'm quite certain I can get into the water, too."

He drew back at the animosity in her voice. "Oh, okay. No sweat. We'll leave you to it, then." Cupping his son's shoulder, he tried to steer him in the direction of the parking lot, but Seth wiggled free and ran back toward Emily.

"Take me with you. Pretty, pretty please? I've never, ever, *ever* been in a boat like that before."

"Seth!" Mark stepped forward, waving his fishing pole. "You can't just invite yourself in someone's boat like that, little man. It's rude."

The boy's shoulders slumped. "I'm sorry," he murmured. "I didn't mean to be rude, Daddy. I really didn't."

Emily dropped to her knees in front of Seth, her black-and-gold bikini top and black spandex shorts evoking a rapid swallow or two on Mark's part. "Maybe your dad can take you out for a few minutes and let you see what a kayak is all about." Peeling her attention from his son long enough to make eye contact with Mark, Emily gestured toward the kayak with her chin. "I've already been out once this evening. Why don't you take him out for a little while?"

"I can't take your boat," Mark protested.

"Sure you can. Have you ever been in a kayak before?" she asked.

He willed himself to focus on her face, to refrain from looking back at her sweet curves, but it was hard. "Kayaks, no. Canoes, yes."

"Then a crash course is in order. Though, since I wasn't expecting this, I don't have a life jacket that'll fit Seth."

"That's okay." Seth raced toward a bag several feet from his castle and tore through its contents, returning with a pair of inflatable armbands. "See? I've got my Floaties!"

Emily made a face. "Not exactly the same thing, I'm afraid. But if you don't go out too far, they'll be okay this one time." Turning to Mark, she said, "And you? What kind of a swimmer are you?"

"Solid."

She considered his response, then gestured toward the boat. "When you sit in a kayak, you need to keep your legs together and your knees slightly bent. Keep your weight over the center line. Remember that and you won't flip."

She retrieved the paddle from the sand. "Now, for locomotion, you grip this with both hands, see?" Placing her hands slightly wider than shoulder width apart, she demonstrated the correct way to hold it and move it. "The blade of the paddle can also be used as a rudder, for steering, if there's somewhere in particular you're trying to go or trying to avoid."

Ten minutes later, Mark knew enough about the boat and the paddle that he was out in the lake with Seth as Emily watched from the shore. "Wow, Daddy! The next time I play castle with my blocks at Gam's house, I'm gonna give my prince and princess a boat just like this."

"You don't think they'd prefer a sailboat or maybe a regular rowboat?" he teased. "Kayaks are kind of narrow and might not fit your princess's dress too well."

"The princess will be fine. She has short dresses, too, you know."

"Oh, I didn't know that." Mark paddled about, glancing back at Emily more than he probably should.

"I like my new friend, Daddy. She's really nice. And she likes castles, too!"

He forced his focus back on his son, noting how the late-afternoon sun was haloing his head. "Oh? You made a new friend at preschool? What's her name?"

"Not at school. Here." The motion of Seth's body as he tried to turn and point toward the shore made the kayak rock. "Whoa! Did you feel that, Daddy?" he asked, wide-eyed.

"I did. And it's because you're moving around. Remember what Emily said about staying in the center?" Mark tilted his chin toward the shore, but knew it was futile, considering Seth was facing forward, his back to him. "So you were talking about Emily just now when you said you made a new friend?"

"She made a flag for my castle!"

Mark had to grin at the enthusiasm in his son's voice. "Wow, you're right. She *is* really nice, huh?"

Seth's head bobbed up and down. "How did you know her name, Daddy?"

*Because once she told me, I couldn't get it out of my head....*

Surprised by the thought, he willed himself to find a more appropriate answer, one that wouldn't get the kayak rocking again. "Remember how I went and played that big-boy game in the woods today? Well, Emily was the teacher."

What Seth said in response, Mark didn't catch, as the mere mention of the beauty on the beach had him glancing over his shoulder once again. She was sitting on the sand, watching their progress. When she spotted him looking, she flashed a thumbs-up.

"Daddy, Daddy, look! Look at that fish!"

At the sudden jerking movement, Mark swung his head back around, but it was too late. Before he was able to reprimand the boy for leaning too far to one side, they were in the water.

Emily jumped up and dived into the lake with record speed. "Are—are you okay?" she called as she stroked toward them.

"Yeah, we're good," Mark assured her, gripping Seth with one hand and the overturned kayak with the other. A moment later he had his son settled safely on his back. "And, oh...remember that tip about staying in the center of the boat? That was a good one," he sputtered through gulps of lake water. "M-maybe you could add a class on kayaking to your company's lineup."

Her laugh cut through the sound of his splashing and warmed him in ways he didn't expect in the chilly water. "I offer kayaking classes all the time, Mark."

Hooking a thumb over his shoulder, he gestured toward his son, who was pretending Mark was a white horse if the words making their way into his left ear were any indication. "We might want to put Seth in the front row of that particular class. So he'd be sure to catch all the helpful little tips you might decide to share."

"I'll keep that in mind," she joked as she stopped momentarily to tread water and take a breath. "How are you holding up?"

"We're fine. My ego, though, hasn't fared quite as well."

"Your secret is safe with me." Nibbling back the full effect of a smile she couldn't hide, Emily swam between Mark and the kayak, her bikini top clinging to her rounded breasts as she flipped the boat right side up. Then, with lithe grace, she hoisted herself into it before he could register much of anything besides how alluring her legs looked as they broke the surface of the water. "Now hand Seth up to me and we've got this."

# Chapter Three

Emily could feel the weight of Mark's stare as she secured the kayak to the roof of her Jeep, his still-labored breath matching her own. She'd felt it as she'd paddled through the water with Seth safely seated between her legs. She'd felt it as Mark had pulled them onto the beach and plucked his son from the boat for a firm yet loving lecture. She'd felt it as they'd stood dripping on the sand, trying to catch their breath. And she'd felt it as she led the way to the car after he insisted on carrying the kayak.

In fact, the only time she wasn't aware of him watching was when she was stealing glances in his direction. But she couldn't help it. Mark Reynolds was easy on the eyes.

"Thanks for making that unexpected swim to help us out. It was above and beyond," he finally said as she hooked the last clip into place. "One minute he was pointing at a fish and the next...well, you know what happened."

She couldn't help it; she laughed. It was either that

or get caught enjoying his dripping, shirtless chest even more than she already was. "Kayaks tend to flip a little easier than canoes. It's why people who are skittish around water tend to shy away from them in favor of a bit more stability."

"Yeah, I get that now." He bent to Seth's level, buying her time to catch her breath. "How about you, little man? You doing okay?"

The boy jumped from foot to foot, the adventure of the past twenty plus minutes further fueling his natural energy. "I had my Floaties on, remember, Daddy?"

She felt Mark's appreciative glance. "And we have Emily to thank for that, don't we?" he continued, his attention trained once again on his son's face. "Did you learn something from that adventure?"

"The lake isn't as warm as the bathtub."

"And…"

Seth's brows furrowed in contemplation. "You should always wear your Floaties?"

"And…"

"Emily is a really good swimmer, just like you, Daddy!"

She tried to cover her ensuing laugh, but Mark's exasperated eye roll made it next to impossible.

"Yes, Emily is a good swimmer. But didn't you also learn that it's better to look at fish from the beach?"

"But I got to get wet!" Seth exclaimed gleefully. "And so did you, Daddy."

A playful smile stretched across Mark's mouth.

"Yeah, but so did Emily. And she'd still be dry if we hadn't commandeered her boat."

"Pizza might make her feel better."

She looked questioningly at Mark as the four-year-old rattled on. "Daddy said we'd go to Sam's for pizza when my castle was all done," he said. "You can come, too, if you want."

"I—I think I better head home, sweetheart." Squatting down in front of him, she pushed a strand of wet hair from his forehead, then tapped the tip of his nose with her finger. "It was very nice to meet you, Seth. You are truly the best sand castle maker I've ever met."

"Please, Emily? The pizza is really yummy. It was my mom's favorite."

Emily tipped her head to afford herself a better view of Mark, noting the hint of sadness in his face at the mention of his late wife. So much about his taking her class made sense now. The drive to check things off one's bucket list always intensified after losing a friend or family member to an early death. It was as if the loss served as a wake-up call about the uncertainty and lack of promises in life. She saw it all the time.

Still, such a loss was hard to rationalize when it came to someone as young as Seth. "That sounds like some extra special pizza if it was your mom's favorite," she finally said.

"It is! Especially the pepperoni kind." Leaning forward, Seth brought his mouth to Emily's ear as if sharing a secret, the excitement in his voice negating any attempt at whispering. "Sometimes, if I smile really big at the waitress lady, she makes the pizza look like a great big smiley face…with funny hair at the top! So please? Won't you come, too? Pretty, pretty please?"

Gesturing at her damp bikini top and drenched shorts, she scrunched up her nose. "I don't think the folks at Sam's Pizza would be too happy to see me in wet clothes."

A snort of disagreement from the boy's father brought a warm flush to her cheeks.

"I'm wet, too. So's my daddy," Seth argued.

"And Sam's has outdoor tables," Mark added.

Slowly she looked from one to the other and back again, the pull for a moment of normalcy making her relent in the end. "Okay. I'm in. It sounds like fun."

Twenty minutes later, any residual worry over wet clothes and disapproving pizza eaters was gone, in its place the kind of happy-go-lucky fun she'd been craving for months. Any tension that came from being huddled so close to Mark evaporated as Seth kept them entertained with tales from his summer preschool program, most of which came back to a castle in some way.

"The other day? At lunch? I built a great big castle out of everybody's *milk cartons*. And then Liam? He's my bestest friend. He made one out of Pixy Stix during playtime," Seth said. "But then Tyler—he's a meany—he came over and kicked Liam's castle down!"

Seth widened his eyes expectantly at Emily and waited.

"You're supposed to gasp at the things Tyler does," Mark whispered in her ear.

"Oh, sorry," she whispered back, before giving the desired response.

Satisfied, Seth continued. "It's okay. Me and Liam, we cast a spell on Tyler."

She glanced at Mark, then back to Seth. "A spell?"

"Uh-huh. And you know what happened?"

Mark paused from taking a drink and narrowed his eyes on his son. "No-o-o…what happened?"

"He got in trouble with Miss Drake. She said she had eyes in back of her head, which means me and Liam are good at casting spells!"

"Then I guess I'd better watch out," Emily declared. "I don't want any eyes in any funny places."

Seth elevated himself onto his knees. "Oh, I wouldn't cast a spell on a princess. That would be bad."

Mark winked at her over the top of his glass before addressing his son once again. "And Emily is a princess, huh?"

"Yupper doodle."

When the pizza arrived and Seth took a break to eat, Mark took over the conversation, peppering her with questions about Bucket List 101 and the clients she'd encountered since starting the business four years earlier.

"When you drew those pictures I saw on your wall, did you know back then that you wanted to teach people how to do all those things?"

She nibbled at the crust of her first piece and then

tossed it on her plate. "Back then, I just knew *I* wanted to do all those things one day. By the time I was halfway through college, I knew I wanted to do them in conjunction with a business."

"Who's your typical client?"

"I'm not sure I have a typical client. People come for all sorts of reasons. Some want to conquer a fear. Some come simply because they love the outdoors. And some, like yourself, are motivated by a personal goal."

Seth pointed at his dad with his slice of pizza. "My mommy taught my daddy not to wait for tomorrow."

Mark drew back. "Where did you get that, little man?"

Turning the pizza toward his mouth, Seth shrugged. "I heard you saying that this morning when you were standing in front of the mirror, trying to decide if you should play in the woods or not."

Emily watched Mark's eyes close only to reopen mere seconds later. "I was talking to myself."

"Then you should be more quiet, Daddy." The little boy took a bite of pizza and started chewing.

"Apparently you're right." Mark looked at Emily with an impish grin. "Nothing like getting a behind-the-scenes look at my many shortcomings, eh?" Suddenly uncomfortable, he grabbed a slice of pizza for himself and raised it in the air like a champagne glass. "Next topic, please…"

Story by story, they ate their way through the rest of a pizza that was every bit as good as Seth had promised.

But it was the time with Mark and Seth that affected Emily most, temporarily filling a void that had been lurking in her soul for years. It was as if Seth's sweet stories and Mark's genuine interest allowed her to pretend, if only for a little bit, that they were her family, sharing the details of their day over dinner.

"You know how to *rock climb?*" Seth asked around a piece of pizza crust bigger than his face.

"It's not polite to talk with food in your mouth," Mark reminded him.

Seth dropped his crust onto his plate. "Do you, Emily?"

Pulling her paper napkin from her lap, she brushed it across her face, then crumpled it into a ball beside her empty glass. "I do."

"Wow!"

"Emily can do all sorts of things." Mark shifted beside her, the brush of his thigh against hers sending a tingle of awareness through her body. "She can pilot a raft through rapids, she can ride a horse through the woods, she can rappel over the side of a mountain and climb huge rocks."

At the naked awe on Seth's face, she turned a playful scowl on the child's father. "You do realize you just made me out to sound like Superwoman, don't you?"

"Nah. Superwoman is a little taller. And her hair is a lot longer. Besides, you're much, *much* better looking."

Mark's words, coupled with the huskiness of his tone, brought her up short. Unsure of what to say, she was more than a little grateful when Seth leaned across the table. "Could you teach me how to rock climb?"

With a steadying breath, she nodded, acutely aware of Mark's hand beside hers. "After you shared such yummy pizza with me, I'd be happy to teach you how to rock climb. If it's okay with your dad, of course."

"Daddy?" Seth's eyebrows rose upward, making both adults laugh out loud. "Please, please? Can Emily teach me how to rock climb?"

A moment of silence had Seth nearly falling out of his seat in anticipation.

"Hmm. If it's okay with Emily, it's okay with me— under one condition."

Bracing herself for the inevitable clean-your-room or put-away-your-toys bribe, she was more than a little surprised—pleasantly surprised, if she was honest with herself—when he revealed his nonnegotiable terms. "I get to learn, too."

Beaming triumphantly, Seth brought his focus back to Emily. "Daddy has this whole week off and I do, too. So we're free tomorrow."

She bit back the laugh Mark was unsuccessful at hiding.

"Oh we are, are we, son?"

"Yupper doodle!"

"Think ten o'clock would work for you?" she asked, with the most serious face she could muster.

Seth hopped down from his seat and consulted his

father in a series of back and forth whispers before repositioning himself at the table. "Ten o'clock works great!"

When the last of the tables around them had been cleared for the night, Mark reached for the check, plunking down thirty bucks and declaring their dinner a delicious success. "Well, little man, I think it's time we walk Emily to her car and give her a big thank-you for rescuing us from the lake and accepting our invitation to dinner."

The little boy moaned. "Do we have to stop eating?"

"We stopped eating an hour ago, when we finished the pizza." Mark pushed his chair back and reached for his son's hand. "Besides, if we want Emily to teach us how to rock climb in the morning, we really should let her go home and get some sleep."

Sensing the boy's reluctance, she took hold of his other hand and gave it a gentle squeeze. "Rock climbing is serious stuff, Seth. You need to be well rested so you can listen extra carefully when I tell you what you need to do."

"Oh. Okay."

They walked through the pizza parlor and out into the night, the answering silence of the crickets marred only by the sound of Seth's flip-flops slapping the pavement. It was a sweet sound, one she'd never really noticed until that moment.

"I had a really nice time tonight, Seth. Thank you for including me—" A shot of pain zipped up her leg, making her drop his hand and reach for the support of a nearby car.

"Emily? Are you okay?"

She smiled through the pain, praying that would wipe the worry from the boy's face. But it didn't work.

In an instant, Mark was at her side, his strong arm slipping around her shoulders and drawing her close. "Hey…talk to me."

As the untimely pain released its grip, she did her best to shrug away the incident. "I'm okay. I just had a quick pain is all."

"Do you get those often?"

Wiggling out from beneath his arm, she did her best to sound nonchalant as she made her way across the parking lot. "Yeah. Well, sometimes, I guess. It's no big deal."

Mark jogged to keep up, her pace quickening as she neared her Jeep. "No big deal? Are you kidding me?" He pointed at the nearest lamppost while studying her face. "Even in this lighting I could see your color drain away."

She shrugged. "It happens from time to time. And it always stops."

"If that happens again, maybe you should call your doctor. You know, to get it checked out or something."

And just like that, the magical spell that had transformed the evening was gone, wiped away by the reality of her life. Turning her back, Emily reached into her purse and pulled out her car keys, her response barely audible to her own ears. "I can't do that."

He took hold of her shoulders and spun her around, raising her chin with his hand. "Why not?"

"Because I can't call him every single time I get a pain. I can't call him every time my arm goes numb. I can't call him every time a bout of fatigue decides to rear its ugly head and confine me to bed for three days. I have a *disease*, Mark. It's life."

MARK TIGHTENED HIS GRIP on the steering wheel and resisted the urge to close his eyes. When he'd picked the multiple sclerosis pamphlet off the floor of Emily's office that morning, it had never dawned on him that it was she who had MS. She was too beautiful, too energetic, too much of a go-getter to have such a debilitating disease.

Yet now that he knew, so many things made sense. The angst she'd exhibited over accepting his business card wasn't denial over a loved one's condition. Her refusal to let him help her with the kayak wasn't some over-the-top display of feminism. And her insistence at racing Seth from the car to the restaurant, even though Mark had pointed to their unexpected dunk in the lake as a reason to take it slowly wasn't about some bottomless well of energy.

No, Emily Todd was angry, and she was determined to show anyone within a stone's throw that she had things under control.

He understood that stage. He'd been there once, too. "Daddy?"

The sound of his son's tiny voice from the backseat derailed Mark's thoughts and forced him to focus on the moment. "What is it, little man?"

"Is Emily gonna die like Mommy did?"

The question was like a punch to his gut, grabbing hold of the arm's-length thoughts and bringing them much too close for comfort. Sneaking a peek at his son's worried face peering at him through the rearview mirror, Mark did his best to change the subject.

"You know what? I think it's time we dust off your bike and start working on getting rid of those training wheels sometime soon. What do you say?"

He released a sigh of relief when the little boy nodded and turned his gaze toward the passing scenery, leaving Mark to his own thoughts once again.

It was still so hard to believe. How could someone who looked like Emily be sick?

*The same way Sally was...*

Just the thought of his late wife brought a lump to his throat. Sally had been so healthy one minute and so sick the next, her all too quick downward spiral made even quicker by the way he'd handled everything. Burying his head in work might have made much of what was happening seem more distant, but it had also robbed him of the little time they had left.

Instead, it was Seth who had been by her side day in and day out, watching his mother slip away until she was gone for good. The memory made Mark sick. What kind of father placed a burden like that on a little boy?

*A coward, that's who...*

Somehow, some way, Mark was going to make things right. He had to. He owed that much to the boy. And to Sally.

But try as he did to engage Seth in conversation for the remainder of the ride home, the worry he'd seen in his son's eyes in the rearview mirror was still there when they returned home. It was there when they'd shared a bowl of ice cream at the kitchen counter. And it was still there when he kissed Seth's forehead and tucked him under the sheets for the night.

Mark had seen that worry in his son's eyes for far too long. He'd watched it eat away at the pure joy that had been Seth's existence prior to Sally's cancer diagnosis. And he'd sat by, virtually paralyzed by his own fear, while that worry had morphed into a steely determination to be what Mark himself seemed incapable of being.

But no more.

Seth had suffered enough for one lifetime.

It didn't matter how hot Emily Todd was. It didn't matter that her enthusiasm and boundless energy breathed life into Mark's stagnant world.

All that mattered was Seth.

All that mattered was keeping his son from ever reliving the kind of grief that had consumed his young life to this point.

Pulling Seth's bedroom door shut behind him, Mark wandered across the hall and into his own room, where the picture of Sally with Seth on his third birthday brought a familiar mist to his eyes.

With fingers that knew the way, he lifted the frame from his nightstand and slowly traced the contours of his wife's face. "His heart is safe with me, Sally," he whispered. "You have my word on that."

# Chapter Four

Emily pressed the intercom button on the side of her phone, working to make her voice sound casual and upbeat. "Trish? Any sign of Mr. Reynolds and his son yet?"

"Still nothing, boss."

"Oh. Okay. Thanks." She pulled her finger back, only to shove it forward once again. "Um, Trish?"

"Yeah, boss."

"My next class is at noon, right?" She glanced at the clock on the wall and noted the rapidly approaching hour.

"Noon it is."

Her shoulders sank along with the tone of her voice. "Okay. Thanks."

With her connection to her assistant broken, Emily pushed back her chair and stood, the enthusiasm that had marked the start of her day giving way to a serious case of unease.

Granted, she didn't know Mark Reynolds all that well. How could she when they'd met just a measly twenty-six hours earlier? But no matter how hard she tried to pin his failure to show up for their first rock-climbing adventure on something as trivial as forgetfulness, she couldn't.

Especially when it had meant so much to his son.

"Seth," she whispered. That was it. Something must have come up with the little boy to cancel their outing and prevent Mark from calling to let her know. It was the only explanation that made any sense.

Perhaps the child was in bed with the flu, or a tummy ache from eating too much pizza the night before. Maybe he'd fallen on the way out to the car that morning and broken his arm, or something crazy like that. Or maybe he'd had a rough night without his mom, and Mark felt it was more important for the little guy to get some rest.

Emily knew it was silly to be so worried about a child she'd just met, but she couldn't help herself. There was something special about Seth, something innocent and pure that spoke to her heart as nothing else had in years.

The fact that he'd been through so much in such a short period of time only served to bolster her gut feeling that Mark wouldn't deny Seth an opportunity to make a new memory unless something fairly serious had intervened.

Her worry at an all-time high, Emily sank back into her desk chair and opened the top drawer. There, where she'd left it, was the card she couldn't get out of her hands fast enough the day before.

Mark Reynolds
Field Worker
Folks Helping Folks Foundation
555-555-5555

Inhaling deeply, she reached for the phone and punched in the number, the final digit quickly followed by a ring that led straight to a nondescript voice mail. When the recording completed its request for her name, number and reason for calling, she obliged, her voice a poor disguise for the worry she wasn't terribly adept at hiding.

"Um…hi. Uh, it's Emily. Emily Todd. From yesterday? At Bucket List 101…and, um, the pizza place?" Realizing she sounded like an idiot, she got to the point, the disappointment she felt over having to wait for a response undeniable. "I got your number from your business card. Could you please give me a call when you get this? Thanks."

She reeled off her phone number, returned the handset to its cradle and then dropped her head into her hands. She'd done everything she could, short of driving back and forth across town trying to guess where Mark and Seth Reynolds lived. All she could do now was wait.

And pray that the images continuing to loop through her thoughts were the by-product of an overactive imagination rather than a spot-on radar that made absolutely no sense where a virtual stranger and his son were concerned.

MARK CROUCHED DOWN beside Laurie's desk and placed a gentle yet firm hand on his son's shoulder. "Now remember what I told you, little man. Miss Laurie has work to do. So it's super important that you sit in this nice seat right here and keep yourself busy, okay?"

Seth nodded.

"And as for me? I'll be in that conference room right there—" he pointed toward the open door just beyond the secretary's desk "—if you have an emergency. But since I just took you to the bathroom, and I'll only be in my meeting for about a half hour, you should be good on that front, right?"

"I'll be good," Seth whispered. "I promise."

Mark reached for the backpack he'd placed beside the chair and unzipped the center compartment to reveal a plethora of activities designed to make the wait as easy on his son—and Laurie—as possible. "I packed your favorite picture books, along with a *Mr. Spaceman* coloring book I managed to score while you were napping at Gam's this afternoon."

At Seth's silence, he reached inside and extracted the new book, flipping it open to reveal page after page of all things space related. "Isn't this the coolest coloring book ever?"

A search of his son's face failed to net the enthusiasm Mark was hoping to see. Disappointed, he tried a different tactic. "If you get hungry, there's an extra yummy cherry lollipop in the front pocket of your backpack that's got your name all over it. Sound good?"

Seth's automatic nod stopped midway as his un-usually dull eyes locked on Mark's. "Daddy? I really would've been a good listener for Emily."

Mark raked a hand down his face before clasping his son's shoulder. "My decision against taking you rock climbing this morning wasn't about listening, little man. It was about keeping you *safe*."

It was a decision he still felt was right even now, some seven hours later. Any residual angst over the whole thing had more to do with his failure to call and cancel their private lesson than anything else.

"Mark? They're ready to start."

He glanced over his shoulder at the woman in her sixties situated behind the gray metal desk. "Thanks, Laurie." Then, turning back to his son, he offered what he hoped was a reassuring smile. "Maybe we can get some ice cream when this is over. How's that sound?"

Seth shrugged. "We have to eat dinner first, Daddy."

Mark didn't know if he should laugh or cry at the sol-emn response more befitting an adult than a four-and-a-half-year-old boy. It made sense, considering everything Seth had been through the past year, but it made Mark all the more protective of his son's childhood.

"Maybe we can make an exception this one time." He brushed a kiss across Seth's head and then stood, his trip to the conference room requiring little more than a stride or two. When he reached the door, he took one last peek at his son, who was still standing in the mid-dle of the foundation's reception area.

"We'll be fine," Laurie assured him. "Now go. The sooner you get in, the sooner you'll be out."

"Thanks, Laurie."

"My pleasure." She swiveled her chair to her computer screen, only to turn back just before he disappeared completely. "Oh, and Mark? A call from a potential client came in for you today. I gave the details to Stan."

"I'll make sure to ask him about it after the meeting." He stepped inside the room and took the empty chair indicated by Stan Wiley, board president of the Folks Helping Folks Foundation. An all-around good guy, Stan made volunteering with the organization a pleasant experience. Stan had gotten involved with the foundation for reasons not dissimilar from Mark's. Regret was a powerful motivator.

"I certainly appreciate everyone coming in on such short notice for a meeting that wasn't on your agenda," Stan began. "But as I told each of you on the phone, it really couldn't be avoided. Not if we want the foundation to be the recipient of a quarter of a million dollars."

A collective gasp rose up around the table.

Stan laughed. "See? I told you this was a meeting worth having."

"Wow. Seriously?"

"That's incredible."

Mark listened to the sentiments of his fellow volunteers, nodding along with each before adding his own.

"That sure is going to open up a lot of possibilities for our clients."

"That's exactly right. And it's why we needed to have this brief meeting. Now that the offer is there, we have to put our heads together and make sure we don't let the money slip out of our grasp." Stan plucked a pile of manila folders from the table in front of him and sent half down each side of the conference table. "That quarter of a million dollars will be the foundation's, provided we meet one very specific and necessary condition stipulated by Jake Longfeld."

Taking the top folder, Mark passed the remaining pile to his left. "Longfeld? As in Longfeld Motors?"

"One and the same," Stan confirmed. "He's been watching the work we've been doing the past few years, and felt it was time to throw one of his always-generous donations in our direction. And we're grateful, of course. But there is this condition we need to find a way to meet."

"Condition?" a woman on the other side of the table repeated.

"That's right." Stan waved his hand. "As you probably know, Jake Longfeld walks with a cane. The reason dates back to an injury he sustained in the armed services some thirty years ago. He's gotten through life just fine in spite of his challenges, but he's wise enough to know that's not the case for everyone with a physical disability, particularly when that disability comes as a result of the kinds of diseases our foundation deals with on a regular basis.

"Which leads me to why we're all here. If you'll open your folders, you'll find a copy of the letter Mr. Longfeld wrote to our foundation, detailing his wishes for his very generous donation. About halfway down the page, you'll see that he wants this money to help two groups near and dear to his heart—those with disabilities, and small business owners."

Mark skimmed the letter from top to bottom, nodding as he did. "So the entire donation doesn't have to go to a small business owner with a disabling disease, just a portion?"

"Exactly," Stan said. "We satisfy that stipulation and we'll be able to help a lot of people."

"Do we have any clients that fit that bill?" a field worker asked.

The president's gaze settled on Mark. "Perhaps." Leaning forward, he flipped through his folder until he came to a pink slip of paper, which he handed to Mark. "A call came in to the foundation for you today, Mark. From a woman named Emily Todd. Ms. Todd owns a small business on the outskirts of Winoka called Bucket List 101. I'm taking it she has physical limitations, if she reached out to us here?"

An image of the petite, pixieish blonde flashed in front of his eyes—the curve of her hips, the sinewy tease of her legs, the tantalizing rise of her breasts, the unforgettable twinkle of her large doelike eyes, the heartfelt smiles she solicited from Seth....

"Mark?"

The sound of his name snapped him back to the present—that and the fact that all eyes in the room were suddenly trained on him. "Uh..."

"Does this woman have physical limitations?" Stan pressed.

He forced himself to address the question, to abandon the image that had him loosening his collar and wishing for a cool glass of water. "At the moment, none that I can see. But with the nature of her disease, that will change."

"Then perhaps we've just met our stipulation."

Stan's words took root. "Wait. Wait. Em—I mean, Miss Todd—isn't a client of ours yet. She, um, well, let's just say she's still in quite a bit of denial about her situation."

"Then I'm counting on you to help her through that stage and onto our client roll." Stan closed his folder and rose to his feet, a triumphant smile making its way across his well-tanned face. "You do that and we can start divvying up the rest of the donation in a way that will enable us to do the most good."

"But I can't force her to seek help," Mark protested.

"She called us, didn't she?" Stan quipped, before adjourning the meeting until the following week. "That fact suggests that our Miss Todd is starting to move toward acceptance at a faster rate than you may have realized."

He leaned his head against the back of the couch and released a long sigh, his dilemma over what to do as worrisome as ever. Sure, there was a part of him that wanted nothing more than an excuse to drive out to Bucket List 101 again and see Emily. There was something about her spark, her spirit, that made him feel more alive than he had in months. But he couldn't ignore the other part, either—the part that wanted to protect his son's heart by keeping her at arm's length.

"Don't get close, don't get hurt," he mumbled under his breath.

It was a good motto. One that would keep him from ever seeing the kind of heart-wrenching ache he'd been unable to erase from Seth's eyes during Sally's illness.

His mind made up, Mark reached for his cell phone and the foundation's volunteer list. Bob McKeon was aces. Clients seemed to really love his gentle, straightforward approach. And with any luck, Emily would feel the same way.

*Emily.*

Once again, the woman who'd captivated his son over a sand castle and a pepperoni pizza flashed before his eyes, causing him to pause, his finger on the keypad of his phone.

Emily was struggling on the first rung of a ladder he knew all too well. He'd seen it in her face when he talked to her about the foundation. He'd heard it in her voice when she'd brushed off his concern about the pain in her leg. And he'd sensed it in the unwavering determination that made her refuse help for even the simplest of things.

She needed a hand.

The kind of hand Seth had given Sally when Mark had been stuck on the same rung as Emily, ignoring reality because he'd thought it would be easier somehow.

But it wasn't.

In fact, in many ways, lingering on that rung had made everything more painful in the end.

The whole reason he'd gotten involved with the foundation was to make up for his selfish behavior during Sally's illness. To push Emily off on Bob when she needed a friendly face and an encouraging word would dishonor the vow he'd made to himself over his wife's grave.

No. Mark wasn't turning his back on people during difficult times. At least, he'd never intended to be that way.

Closing the phone, he tossed it onto the coffee table, the determination he'd once prided himself on prior to Sally's illness and death returning for the first time in entirely too long.

*He* would talk to Emily. *He* would help her reach the next rung of the ladder, by convincing her to accept assistance from the foundation. And he would do that for her just as he would for any other potential client.

Because that's what she was, what she *needed* to be.

For Seth's own good.

# Chapter Five

Emily was just wrapping up a class on outdoor survival when Mark walked in, his tall, well-built form commanding attention and drawing the heads of all three female students in his direction. A quick search of his face and stance turned up nothing to indicate there was trouble at home. But still, not to call? Something had to have come up.

In a flash, Mark was at her side, his hand on her arm, his husky voice in her ear. "Are you okay?"

Feeling the questioning eyes of her students, she yanked free of his grip, dropping her voice to a whisper. "What the hell do you think you're doing?"

He stepped back as if he'd been slapped. "You were in pain again. I saw it in your eyes just now."

"Pain? I wasn't in any..." Her words trailed off as she put two and two together, then turned to address the three women and four men who had just taken the first of four classes designed to teach them how to survive in the wild. "I want to thank all of you for such a fun and energetic class today. Hopefully I answered all of your great questions and that you're looking forward to next week's class as much as I am."

A muted chorus of agreement rang out as all seven made their way toward the door, several of them stopping to glance back first at Mark and then Emily, the unease on their faces igniting her fury all over again.

When they were safely out of the room and down the hall, she turned back to him. "How dare you make my students doubt my ability to run this class!"

"Doubt your ability? Where on earth did you get— wait. Wait just a minute. I didn't do that," he protested. "I just wanted to make sure you were okay."

"By making a production in front of them? About pain I wasn't having? Oh, okay." She heard the sarcasm in her voice and forced her mouth closed over the rest of her rant.

He stared at her and then broke left and began pacing around the classroom. "But I saw the flash of pain in your eyes when I walked into the room."

She rested her hands on her hips. "That wasn't pain. It was *worry*."

He stopped midstep and met her eyes. "Okay. And I get that. It's why I'm here, actually." He lifted his left hand to brandish some colorful brochures featuring the same logo as the business card he'd given her two days earlier. "We got your call at the foundation and we're so glad that you're reconsidering the idea of accepting help from us. These pamphlets will give you an idea of the kinds of things we can do to help—"

"You're here because of the message I left on your voice mail?"

"Yes."

She brought her hands to her cheeks and worked to steady her breathing, the meaning behind Mark's statement becoming crystal clear. "I didn't call because I want some sort of help from your foundation," she snapped.

His eyebrows rose. "Then why did you call?"

"Why did I call?" she echoed in a tone that was bordering on shrill. "Hmm, I don't know. Maybe I was *worried?*"

"About what?" he asked.

"Not what, *who.*" She kept her focus firmly on his face as she filled in the blanks he was so obviously missing. "As in worried about Seth. And you."

"You were worried about Seth and me? But why?"

She considered turning her back on him and simply walking away, but opted instead to have her say. "Maybe because I saw the way his face lit up when we agreed on a time for our first rock-climbing adventure, which should have had the two of you walking through that door yesterday morning." Sure enough, the color drained from his face as she continued, his genuine cluelessness over his faux pas making her even angrier. "I know what kind of dad you are. I'd be an idiot not to see that. So I think it's fairly understandable why I'd chalk up your no-show to something being wrong, instead of just you blowing off a promise you made to your kid."

Taking two steps backward, he sank into a chair and raked a hand across his face. "And so you called the foundation to see if we were okay?"

"It was the only number I had."

He closed his eyes momentarily, only to open them again with obvious hesitation. "Oh, man. I'm sorry, Emily. I didn't realize…"

Feeling her anger edge toward an unexplained sadness, she waved his words aside. "Look, just tell me he's okay. Beyond that, I don't need or want to hear anything else."

Mark's eyes stopped just shy of meeting hers. "He's fine. We just, um, had other things to do."

"Other things to do," she repeated, as if hearing the words out of her own mouth would somehow take the sting out of them. It didn't.

And it was her own fault. So they'd talked on a beach—big deal. So they'd laughed together for hours over pizza—big deal. So Seth had seemed to respond to her as strongly as she did to him—big deal. It had been one evening—one measly two or three hours.

The fact that she'd given the encounter a second thought, let alone allowed it to excite her while simultaneously meaning so little to the man sitting in front of her, was embarrassing.

She turned toward the door. "Well, I'm sorry you drove all the way out here just to inform me you had better things to do yesterday than show up for a class *you* scheduled. Take care of yourself, and say hi to Seth for me."

"Emily, wait. It's not what you think."

She stopped. "And you know what I'm thinking now, too?"

"Yeah. That I'm an insensitive jerk."

She opened her mouth, only to shut it without uttering a word. Really, why argue the truth?

"But it's not like that. Not in the way that you think, anyway." The legs of Mark's chair scraped against the linoleum floor as he rose to his feet and closed the gap between them. "I decided to refrain from coming here with Seth yesterday because of him. Or, rather, *for* him, actually."

"I don't understand." She dropped her hands to her hips again. "Your son was beside himself with excitement at the pizza place just thinking about learning how to climb. How could your decision not to show up be for him?"

Mark shifted foot from foot to foot, clearly uncomfortable with their discussion. "I—I can't allow him to hurt like he has this past year. Not knowingly, anyway. To do so would make me a pretty crappy dad."

"Teaching him how to rock climb would make you a crappy dad?" she asked in confusion, just as some semblance of a reason hit home. "Is this about safety? Because if it is, you have to believe I know what I'm doing.

Teaching these kinds of skills is my job, Mark. It's how I make my living. He would have been perfectly safe."

An awkward and all-too-telling pause caught her by surprise.

"Wait a minute. Please don't tell me you doubt my ability because I have MS?"

For a moment, she didn't think he was going to answer, but in the end he did, his words suddenly making it difficult for her to breathe. "It's not your ability in light of the MS that I'm worried about, Emily."

"Then what?" she whispered.

"It's the threat your condition wields over my son's heart."

"Your son's heart? What on earth are you talking about?"

She watched as Mark walked aimlessly around the room, clenching and unclenching his hands. When he finally turned to face her, the pain in his eyes was like a lightning bolt to her chest, swift and unmistakable. "Most three-year-olds spend their days playing. Girls with their dolls, and boys with their cars and trucks. When they grow tired of that, they retire to a couch to watch their favorite show on TV, snacking on a hot-from-the-oven chocolate chip cookie with a tall glass of cold milk and a straw. It's the way it's supposed to be, you know?"

Without waiting for a response she was at a loss to provide, he continued, his words, his tone, taking on the emotion evident on his face. "Seth didn't have that. Not beyond his first three years, anyway. No, *Seth's* play-time was spent in medical offices and hospital rooms. And instead of watching cartoon characters chasing each other all over the television screen, he watched his mom grow sicker and sicker, and sicker until she slipped from his life completely."

Swallowing over the lump that grew in her throat, Emily took a step forward. "Oh, Mark, I'm so sorry. I didn't realize just how awful it was for the two of—"

He held up his hands, cutting her off. "I can't take that experience away from him. I can't go back and air-brush out all his pain and anguish, regardless of how much I wish I could. But what I *can* do is protect the rest of his childhood. Keep him from having to go through something like that ever again."

Suddenly the reason the pair had failed to show the day before was as plain as the nose on her face. And she didn't like it one bit.

"Wait, please. Are you telling me you didn't want to bring him here to *rock climb* with me because you're afraid I'm going to die on him like his mother did?"

Mark's glance at the floor was all the answer she needed.

"First of all, a quick fact check. I have multiple scle-rosis. And while MS can be a debilitating disease, the likelihood that it's going to kill me is slim to none. Will it shorten my life? Maybe, but only by about five per-cent. *Five percent.* The chance I'll die being run over by a bus in downtown Winoka is probably higher than that."

Slowly he lifted his head. "But—"

"And second, Seth barely knows me. I mean, c'mon, you really think a few hours at a pizza parlor and a few more spent learning to climb rocks would leave him so enamored with me that he'd be seriously impacted by some unexpected decline in my health? Because I certainly don't—"

"Didn't you see how taken he was with you at the pizza place? How he hung on every word out of your mouth? How he tried to endear you to him with the best knock-knock jokes making the rounds of his summer preschool program? Didn't you see how he looked at you with such awe and genuine happiness? Because *I* did, and it took my breath away."

At her quiet gasp, Mark continued, his voice growing raspier by the second. "But that wasn't all. I also felt his fear when he asked about your illness on the way home that night. It was...*crushing.*"

She blinked at the tears that threatened to cut paths down her cheeks. "He was afraid? Of me?"

"He was afraid *for* you. And trust me when I say that kind of fear is worse, far worse." Mark tipped his head back and looked up at the ceiling, the nature of the conversation, coupled with the countless memories it surely dragged to the surface, sapping him of physical energy. "I don't care how perfect that smile of his was the other night when he looked at you. It's not worth watching him hurt the way he did with his mom. Not for me, anyway."

IT WAS QUICK. Fleeting, even. But he'd seen it as surely as if a chorus of angels had underscored its presence.

Emily was taken by Seth, too.

The knowledge made Mark pause and search for a softer, easier way to get his feelings across. But before he could utter another word, the moment was gone.

"So why show up now if you didn't have the guts to call and tell me all of this yesterday morning? Surely you could have popped your precious pamphlets in the mail and saved yourself the trip."

He looked down at the brochures he'd forgotten he had, and held them out to her once again. "Because I—I wanted to talk to you. To see if I could convince you to let the Folks Helping Folks Foundation help you through this difficult time."

"There is no difficult time," she said through clenched teeth before sweeping her hands toward her body. "Look at me. Do you really think I'm having a difficult time?"

"Maybe not now, but down the road—maybe. Probably. But that's why I'm here. That's why I'm trying to tell you about the foundation. We can equip your house and your office with the things you might need later, like a wheelchair ramp or a special tub for your bathroom that will protect you from slipping." Realizing she wasn't going to take the brochures, he dropped them onto the nearest desk. "In fact, the foundation stands to get a very large donation if we can find a local business owner who can benefit from our work. And since this—" he spread his arms and gestured around the room "—is your business, we thought maybe—"

Her eyes narrowed. "Oh. I get it now."

He rushed to soothe away any misunderstanding. "Wait. It's not like that. You know I wanted to help you the other day, long before I knew a thing about this donation."

"Right. Only now it's even more important to pressure me into something I don't want because my…my *disease* helps you and your precious foundation put a checkmark in some stupid little box." She pivoted and paced across the room, stopping when she reached the far wall. "I'm fine, Mark. Just fine. Find someone else to help you tick off your boxes."

"But you have a debilitating disease. You said so yourself."

For the briefest of moments he actually thought she was going to come back and smack him. Instead, she raised her hand and beckoned to him.

Scooping up the brochures, he followed her from the classroom and down the same corridor as two days earlier. When he reached her office, he stepped inside.

She grabbed an overstuffed album from a nearby shelf and slammed it onto her desk. With a flick of her wrist, she snapped back the cover to reveal page upon page of news clippings and pictures highlighting her many outdoor skills. "Can you climb a tree that looks like that?" she asked, pointing at a photo of her near the top of a blue spruce. "And how about this?" She turned to the next page. "Can you scale the side of a mountain, Mark?"

There was lots more of the same—Emily paddling through stage four rapids. Dangling from the edge of a cliff. Jumping over a series of fallen trees, bareback on a horse. Scuba diving and waving at an underwater camera. And all the while, no matter what she was doing, she was looking incredible.

He swallowed once, twice. "No. I'm afraid I can't."

She pushed the album shut and turned to face him, her lips lusciously plump as they parted to dress him down once again. "I may have MS, Mark," she hissed. "But MS doesn't have me."

Reaching out, he cupped his free hand around the back of her head and pulled her close, the intoxicating feel of her soft hair giving way to the reality that was her mouth—warm, enticing and oh so exciting.

When her lips parted to allow access to his probing tongue, he pulled her still closer, their bodies melding against one another effortlessly until the ring of her phone snapped them both back to reality.

She stepped away, her eyes glazed, her voice breathless. "I have to get that. Trish is out today." Without waiting for a response, she grabbed the receiver. "Bucket List 101. This is Emily."

Mark took the reprieve offered by the call to get his

body under control, the intensity of their kiss making his thoughts run in a direction not conducive to their present setting. Never mind the fact that he barely knew her....

"Oh, hi, Kate. Yeah, yeah, I'm fine. Really. I don't know why you think my voice sounds funny. I was just a little busy, that's all."

He tried to give her privacy, to refrain from eavesdropping on the one-sided conversation, but it was hard. Especially when he'd always been sort of good at lip reading, and he couldn't seem to keep his gaze off her kiss-swollen lips....

"Yes, yes, I'm still coming." She glanced in his direction, focusing on his face for mere seconds before taking in the clock over his head. "No, I didn't realize how late it was getting. I'll be there in fifteen minutes. Uh-huh. Yeah. Okay. I'll see you then."

Slowly, she lowered the phone to its base, her cheeks crimson. "That was my friend Kate. The one who found all of—" she turned and pointed at the framed childhood drawings that had captivated him the day they met "—*those*. Anyway, I was due at her house for a barbecue thirty minutes ago and, well, I'm late."

"Can I come?" he asked, before realizing what he was saying. But instead of retracting the bold question, he let it stand, buoyed by the memory of her lips on his.

"Don't you have to get home to Seth?" she asked.

"Seth is spending the evening with my mother. He

won't be home until late tomorrow, probably after dinner."

Emily opened her mouth to speak, but closed it again when he reached for her hand, his voice husky with the kind of emotion he knew he'd have to dissect later—when he was alone.

"Please, Emily? I'd like to go with you."

# Chapter Six

The second they looped around the side of the house and into Kate's line of vision, Emily knew she'd made a mistake.

To bring a guy who looked like Mark to a barbecue with a heavy concentration of couples versus singles was bound to raise a few eyebrows under any circumstances. Add the fact that it was Kate—a woman who bemoaned Emily's single status on a regular basis—who was throwing the barbecue and, well, she was doomed.

"Emily! You're here!" Her friend disengaged herself from a small group of people Emily recognized from the Memorial Day barbecue Kate and her husband had thrown six weeks earlier, and met them just inside the hedge that bordered the east side of the couple's property. Extending her hand, Kate widened her eyes at Emily and then beamed up at Mark. "Hi, I'm Kate. Emily and I have known each other since our finger painting days."

His laugh was strong and sure. "And I'm Mark.

Emily and I have known each other since she stuck a compass in my hand and tried to lead me astray in the woods three days ago."

"I didn't lead you astray," she protested. "I gave you the same coordinates as everyone else. You just seemed to be a little distracted in the beginning, that's all."

He swept his hand in her direction, making her keenly aware of the white skirt and powder-blue tank top she'd donned that morning, knowing her day would be spent in a classroom rather than in the woods or on the lake. "Who knew I had to focus on the compass?" he quipped to Kate with a wink for good measure.

Emily felt her mouth gape, and worked to compose herself even as her friend's eyes crackled with the kind of excitement that left her own stomach in knots.

*Great.*

"Come. Come. You have to meet my husband, Joe." Looping her arm through Mark's, Kate fairly dragged him across the French patio and over to the pickup game of basketball taking place on the other side of the yard between Joe and an eight-year-old guest. "Joe and I met in high school. He was distracted by me when we crossed paths at the diner."

Hoping the lump in the pit of her stomach was a by-product of hunger rather than her shortsighted concession in bringing Mark to the barbecue, Emily headed over to the food table, her history with Kate filling in the rest of the story Mark was no doubt hearing. It was one she knew well, considering that she had been sitting at the same table in the now infamous local hangout when Joe had walked in with four of his buddies from the basketball team that fateful day. The second Kate and Joe had spotted one another across the restaurant, their romantic fate had been sealed.

But it hadn't worked that way for Emily. Ever.

Sure, she'd dated her fair share of guys throughout high school, college and beyond, but none of them had ever quite reached the bar she'd set for someone who would be her life's mate. No, that person had to be smart, funny, motivated, creative and outdoorsy. He had to enjoy conversation and silence. And he had to look at her as if she was someone special.

*Like Mark had just now when he was telling Kate about the orienteering class….*

Emily stilled her hand over the bowl of pretzels and shook her head. Oh, no. She would not allow Kate's you-need-to-find-your-soul-mate-and-you-need-to-find-him-now mantra start playing in her head.

Four out of five goals was good enough. Especially in light of her illness.

"Em, he's gorgeous. Gor-geous. I am so, so, *so* happy for you."

She swatted away her gushing friend with a handful of pretzels before popping one in her mouth and removing herself from the earshot of a few other guests.

"What?" Kate persisted, staying on her heels. "Am I wrong? Is Mark not gorgeous?"

Lifting her hand to block the sun, Emily scanned the

backyard until her friend's outstretched finger pointed the way to the basketball court and the game that had grown to include five men and the eight-year-old. Even from where she was standing she couldn't help but enjoy the view.

Mark Reynolds was truly a fine-looking man. His hair, which had caught her attention from the start with its rich brown color, was the kind a woman could get her fingers lost in. His smile, whether flashed in her direction over a piece of pizza, or accompanying some good-natured trash talk, as was the case at that moment, was of the knee-weakening variety if she'd ever seen one. And his chiseled jawline...

She closed her eyes, popped a second and third pretzel into her mouth, and then opened her eyes again, this time honing in on her closest friend. "Yes, he's attractive—I'd have to be an idiot not to see that. But I'm not interested."

Kate's left eyebrow rose. "Not interested? Are you nuts?"

"He's just someone I know. Barely." At Kate's foot tapping, she continued. "He stopped by the office today to drop off some, um, paperwork I didn't need, and I felt sorry for him. So I invited him along. No big deal. Really."

The right eyebrow rose alongside the left. "And dinner at Sam's Pizza, what was that?"

Emily pulled her focus back from the basketball court where it had strayed once again, seemingly independent of her brain and the conversation she was trying to have and discard. "He told you about Sam's?"

Kate grinned so widely that Emily actually found herself glancing at the patio for evidence of any canary feathers her friend may have swallowed. "He did."

Emily folded her hands across her chest. "And did he happen to tell you the only reason I went at all is because his son was so insistent and I didn't have the heart to say no?"

"His son?" Kate sputtered. "He has a son?"

"Seth is four and a half. And if you saw him, and he'd asked *you* to come along for pizza, you'd have gone, too. Trust me."

Turning her head, Kate looked back at the court. "So he's divorced, then?"

"No, he's a widower. His wife died sometime in the last six months or so."

"He sure seems happy to be here with you."

She had to laugh at that. "You mean playing basketball with your husband, right?"

"Have you not seen how many shots he's missed since we've been standing here?"

"So maybe he's not a basketball guy, Kate. Believe it or not, those do exist. Difficult to fathom, I know. But still…"

Her friend made a face. "I know that. But I also know he *is* a basketball guy, based on what he told Joe when I introduced them."

"Maybe he lied," she quipped, shrugging.

"Or maybe he's spending more time looking over at you rather than focusing on the game."

"Kate. Please." She heard the exasperated tone in her voice, saw the heads of several people turn toward them as a result. Gritting her teeth, Emily tried her best to get a handle on her increasing agitation before every eye in the place was trained in her direction. "We're just *friends*. That's it."

Without waiting for the retort she was quite sure would come, she headed back to the food table and a recently added plate of brownies. She was about to reach for one when Mark appeared at her side, breathing heavily.

"The...game just...ended so Joe could start on the burgers and dogs. So what do you say we...we check out that horseshoe pit...over there—" he gestured toward the back edge of the property "—while he cooks? That way...maybe I can...catch my breath a little."

For a moment, she considered declining. To accept would mean giving Kate another reason to keep needling her. But in the end, Emily agreed. After all, with any luck, Joe would need Kate's help at the grill and her friend would finally turn her attention to something else.

One could hope, anyway.

"I'm in," Emily said, grabbing one last handful of pretzels from the bowl at the end of the table. "Anything to get out from under this scrutiny for a little while."

"Scrutiny?" Mark echoed. "What kind of scrutiny?"

Oops. She hadn't meant to share that thought aloud. She simply shrugged. "Never mind. Let's go."

HE TRIED TO FOCUS on the game, he really did. But it was hard. Damn hard.

Emily was the kind of girl who would make cars swerve off roads when she went jogging down a busy street. She just was. But what took his own first swerve all the way into a tree with no hope of recovering was the fact that her beauty was only part of the story. She was also smart and engaging, with a completely unpretentious and slightly self-deprecating manner where her looks and her body were concerned.

Her physical prowess, however, was a different matter. That, she took pride in. Not a boastful kind, but rather a self-satisfied one. As if she'd worked hard to learn certain skills and didn't feel the need to hide her ability in those areas from anyone.

"It's your toss, Mark."

In fact, she was so skilled at so many things, he found himself wanting to start stretching his own limits a little. See what he could do, too...

"Earth to Mark... Come in, Mark."

The repeated sound of his name brought him back to the moment. "I'm sorry?"

Emily pointed to the horseshoe in his hand. "It's your toss."

"Oh, yeah." He pulled his arm back and then swung it forward, his horseshoe sailing through the air and landing a full twelve inches from its target. "Wow. That was lame." Her laugh tingled down his spine and brought an answering smile to his own face. "You think that's funny, eh?"

She held up her hands and gave them a little shake. "I shouldn't be laughing. Don't mind me."

"Like it's easy to ignore the woman who's beating your pants off at horseshoes." Before she could respond, he moved on, tackling a subject he'd been wondering about since they'd arrived. "So tell me…why aren't you married or coupled off, like most of your friend's guests seem to be?"

Emily launched her last horseshoe at the target, the sound of metal on metal bringing another smile to the lips he couldn't seem to forget kissing. "Well, that's a bit of a loaded question, don't you think?"

"Sorry. I didn't mean to come across as nosy. I guess I just can't fathom why you haven't been snatched up by at least a dozen different guys by now."

Shrugging, she wandered over to a pair of Adirondack chairs nestled beneath a large oak tree and claimed one as her own. "It's okay. I don't really mind. I guess I'm just on edge about that particular topic, thanks to Kate."

He took the other chair. "She's a little pushy where your love life is concerned, huh?"

For a moment, he was afraid he'd offended Emily again, but when she finally answered, her words painted a very different picture. "Kate is one of those people who has a life plan. One that's actually written out on a piece of paper. All the goals she wants to hit are spelled out right there, in order, with bullets. Last I checked, she was on number six, I think."

"Number six?"

Emily nodded, her gaze fixed on the trunk of the oak tree. "The sixth bullet point. Which, between you and me, means she's trying to have a baby. It could be a girl or a boy this first time around. But whatever it is will necessitate a specific gender where bullet point number seven is concerned. Because she's supposed to have one of each, you know, according to her life plan."

"A life plan? Really?"

"Uh-huh. And Kate believes the things on her list are the same ones everyone else is supposed to want. You know…get married, work for a few years, develop a few hobbies, have a child, and so on and so on. It's why she's having a little difficulty accepting the fact that my life has taken a very different path. And while sometimes I think she gets it—at least in a grudging way—there are other times where I actually feel as if I've disappointed her."

"By not getting married?" he asked. "Come on, I can't believe that's true. Besides, there's still plenty of time for you to hit a few bullet points of your own. Lots of women these days wait to get married into their early thirties and beyond. Sally and I just did it a little early. More like Kate and Joe." He silently cursed the way his tone softened at the mention of his late wife, afraid that

Emily would jump on the same apology bandwagon his friends rode and pull him from the place he was at that moment....

With Emily.

"I guess that's it. But as I try to tell her all the time, sometimes plans change. And that doesn't always have to be a bad thing, right?"

Silence enveloped them as they slipped into their own thoughts—his about the events he hadn't anticipated when he'd met and married Sally, and hers about things he could only guess at.

"Come and get it before it's gone!" Joe bellowed from the grill. "Got plenty of burgers and hot dogs for everyone. But if you snooze, be prepared to lose, folks."

Despite the answering rumble of his stomach, Mark found himself wishing for another moment or two alone with Emily. There was something about her quiet confidence that made him feel alive—a feeling that had been sporadic at best since Sally's diagnosis, illness and subsequent funeral. Maybe part of it was simply having the chance to talk about something other than his wife's death and how Seth was coping—subjects few of his friends seemed capable of deviating from these days. More than that, though, was the growing attraction Mark felt for the woman seated by his side. Stealing a glance in her direction, he searched for a way to put a smile back on her face. "Hey, what do you say we grab something to eat and have a rematch? And this time I'll actually *try*."

Her eyes crackled to life. "Are you implying I only beat you because you weren't trying?"

"I'm not implying that, I'm saying that," he teased.

"Oh, okay. But just so you know, you might want to go easy on the trash talk, mister. Because if you don't, you may find yourself eating way more than one of Joe's famous burgers by the time we're done."

"You think so?"

"I know so," she quipped.

Sure enough, two hamburgers, one corn on the cob, a hearty helping of potato salad and three losses later, he collapsed onto the same Adirondack chair he'd sat on earlier. Only this time, instead of stealing glances at Emily and hesitating over which way the conversation should go, he was interacting with her as if they'd known each other for years. She laughed at his corny jokes, teased him about his less-than-stellar horseshoe skills and smiled at him as if she was every bit as aware of the sparks flying between them as he was. And it felt good. Undeniably good.

All too soon, however, dusk gave way to darkness and Mark found himself reluctantly conceding that it was time to call it a night. His hand found the small of her back as they made their way around the side of the house and headed toward her car. "Emily, I had a really great time tonight. I can't tell you the last time I did something like this. Except, of course, the other night."

Her feet slowed as they approached the Jeep. "You were at a barbecue the other night?"

"No, I was at Sam's. With you." A nearby streetlamp cast an alluring glow across her face, and he swallowed.

"Then I don't get it. Did something like what?"

He looked to the sky, taking in the crystal-clear view of the stars above. It had been so long since he'd allowed himself simply to breathe, without traveling down the familiar road of should-haves and could-haves where the past eighteen months were concerned. When he was ready, he allowed himself to look at her again, noting the way her skirt clung to her ass in a sweet yet flirty kind of way, and how the tops of her breasts peeked out along the upper edge of her halter top.

"Like have fun. Like laugh. Like…*live*."

Reaching out, he traced the side of her face with his fingertips, drawing her in for a kiss that had his heart accelerating in a way no pickup game of basketball ever could.

## Chapter Seven

If it weren't for an approaching car, Emily could have stayed in Mark's arms all night, tasting his lips, marveling at the sensation of their mingling tongues and feeling the heat of his growing excitement against her body. She disengaged herself far slower than circumstances called for, resulting in some rubbernecking from the teenage occupants inside.

She stepped back, swiping at her lips in an unexpected burst of shyness that brought a crinkling to the skin around Mark's eyes. "I—I…wow. I don't know what to say," she confessed, once the car had passed.

"Say you don't want to call it quits for the night yet. Say we can hang out a little longer. Say I don't have to stop kissing you for at least another couple of hours."

Lifting her wrist into the glow of the streetlamp, she took note of the time, her heart sinking at the late hour. "But it's already eleven o'clock and—"

"It's a Friday, remember?"

She paused. Mark was right. There was no pressing need to get home, other than to take her medication.

And that could wait another couple of hours if necessary. In fact, the notion of not allowing her condition to impact her evening in any way was very appealing.

"So what do you suggest?" she finally asked, the resulting smile on his face warming her from head to toe.

"I don't know. But I'll think of something."

She savored the feel of his hands on her hips as he leaned against the car and pulled her close, the look in his eyes as he stroked her cheek threatening to render her speechless if she didn't think fast. "What about a little preview of what you missed the other morning?"

"What I missed?" he asked absentmindedly, as his hand moved to her hair and then her neck.

"The back entrance to my office opens to a room two stories tall. The climbing walls I have in there aren't quite the same as scaling the side of a mountain, but they're perfect for someone wanting to learn. If you're interested, that is."

"Are you serious?"

"Sure. It'll be fun." She disengaged herself from his arms and pointed her key at the car, the quick chirp-chirp of the locks accompanied by a flash of the headlights. "I've got a pair of shorts and a T-shirt I can change into at my office. Then we're good to go."

He stopped en route to the passenger side and made a T with his hands. "Whoa. But I like the outfit you're wearing now."

"I can't rock climb in a skirt, Mark."

"Darn."

She laughed. "I can put it back on when we're done. Though why it'll matter at midnight or later is beyond me."

"Because you look spectacular, that's why."

She slid behind the steering wheel and put the key in the ignition, the purr of the engine, coupled with the intensity in Mark's eyes, making her more than a little nervous. She'd gone rock climbing hundreds of times. She'd taught men of all shapes and sizes how to do the same on the very wall they'd be scaling in under twenty minutes. Yet in that moment, she would have second-guessed her ability to teach someone their ABC's, let alone how to climb a two-story wall, with her heart thudding in her chest the way it was.

And she knew why.

For as much as she bemoaned Kate's life plan, Emily wasn't much different herself. She might not have made an actual bullet-point list designed to take her from college to her death bed, with a nod to every major milestone in between, but she *did* like to be prepared.

It was why, she always suspected, she liked the kind of activities she'd built her life around. To kayak, she needed to be prepared—with a paddle and a life jacket. To take a survival trip through the woods, she needed to be prepared—with things like flint and a knife. To rock climb, she needed to be prepared—with rope, a harness and connectors. To scuba dive, she needed to be prepared—with a diving helmet and suit, weights, a regulator and a tank.

And when the doctor had walked into her hospital room six months earlier and uttered the words *multiple sclerosis,* she'd begun the mental preparation necessary to abandon all hope for her fifth and final childhood dream—of becoming a wife and mother. She'd prepared herself for living alone. For finding things that would fulfill a life shared by no one.

But Mark Reynolds, and the way he looked at her as if she was someone special, was throwing a monkey wrench in those plans.

"You do know that, right?"

She peered at him across the center console and shook her head. "I'm sorry, Mark. I think I may have missed what you just said."

"Is something wrong?" he asked.

"No. But I zoned out there for a minute." She slid the gearshift to Drive and pulled the car from the curb, the motion a welcome reprieve from the thoughts she was having at that moment. "So what is it I'm supposed to know?"

"That you look spectacular."

And just like that, the thoughts were back. Mark Reynolds hit every single one of the must-haves she'd set for a mate. He was smart, funny, motivated, out-doorsy—all of it. He was, essentially, a no-brainer, as Kate was fond of saying about all sorts of things in life. But the problem wasn't him. Or even the notion of him. It was Emily.

Sure, she wanted to believe there was hope that

someone would love her despite her condition. But the recurring nightmare she had three or four times a week said otherwise. It didn't matter how supportive her face-less prince tried to be, because the part that woke her in a cold sweat was having her prince slowly giving up his own wants and needs to be her caretaker.

"I'm guessing by your silence that you don't know that. So let me be the one to tell you that you do. And as I always tell Seth, I'm a pretty smart guy when it comes to the easy stuff in life."

She had to laugh. "Isn't *everyone* smart when it comes to the easy stuff?"

"You don't get out much, do you?" Mark quipped. "Then again, who am I to make a statement like that? I *never* get out."

His comment hit her like a slap to the side of the head. Tonight wasn't about looking inward. It was about having fun.

Mark needed that.

And so, too, did she.

Pulling her office keys from her purse, she climbed out of the Jeep and gestured for Mark to follow. "C'mon, let's go."

When they reached the main door of the barn, she unlocked it and stepped inside, the motion-sensor light she'd mounted in the hallway switching on instanta-neously. "Why don't you head downstairs, and I'll join you as soon as I get changed."

"Don't take too long, okay?"

"I won't." And she didn't. Less than five minutes later she was standing with him at the base of the climbing wall, with a harness for each of them. Dropping one to the ground, she helped Mark into his and connected it to his rope. "Take your time. This wall here—" she touched the one directly in front of them "—is the beginner wall. Your hand- and footholds are closer together on it. Once you've mastered this section, you can move on to the intermediate wall, where the hand- and footholds are farther apart and the climb is a bit more challenging."

"What about that wall?" Mark asked, pointing to the far side of the room.

"That's the expert wall. We'll save that for another day."

Mark snorted. "Or maybe another year."

She secured herself into her own harness and hooked herself in as Mark's belay. "No, another *day*. You'll get this, if you try. The folks who don't are the ones who let fear slow them down. Then the doubts take over and knock them the rest of the way out. I see it all the time. But if you think about it, climbing a wall or scaling the side of a mountain is really no different than wanting to write a novel or become a world champion chess player. You just have to check your hang-ups at the door and do what needs to be done to make it happen.

"As for what you need to do here, keep your body close to the wall. People tend to think their knees should be pointed inward, but if you turn them out a little bit, you'll be much more successful."

When she was done sharing a few more true tips, she motioned toward the wall. "Now it's time for you to give it a go. I'll be your belay a few times, then I'll hook you up to one of the electronic ones."

HOLD BY HOLD, Mark moved higher, Emily's advice about turning his knees outward helping immeasurably. His first trip up the wall was about trial and error, his second time solely about improvement. But by the third trip, he'd discovered that the best way to move was to do it in two parts—first his limbs, then his weight. Employing that technique again and again ensured this was his most skillful effort yet.

He glanced down over his shoulder as he hit the bell at the top of the wall, Emily's enthusiastic praise bringing an even bigger smile to his face. "Think I'm ready to move on to the next wall?" he called down.

"Absolutely. But you need to know that the chance of falling increases as the holds decrease in number." When he reached the bottom, she unhooked him from the rope and led him over to the intermediate wall, where she proceeded to hook him in once again. "Now, if you feel yourself start to slip, you need to push away from the wall right away. If you keep your feet out in front of you as the rope comes tight, you can brace yourself and keep from hitting the wall as you swing inward. Okay?"

"Feet out, push away...got it." He moved toward the wall, only to stop as he reached the base. "Is this your favorite?"

She shook her head and pointed to the wall behind them. "I like the expert wall best."

Now that he knew a bit more about the sport, he took a closer look, finding the distance between each hold far more impressive than he'd first realized. "Actually, I was asking more about rock climbing as opposed to the other sports you do. Is it your favorite?"

Her eyes widened with an excitement he envied, and he found himself hanging on her every word, her enthusiasm for exploration and life in general transforming her already beautiful face into something truly captivating.

"Wow. That's a tough one to answer. I like climbing because of the challenge. Being out on a real mountain, it's almost like a puzzle. You have to figure out the best hold to get you to the next level." She wandered across the room and took a seat on the bottom step of a narrow riser. "Rafting is exhilarating. One minute everything is calm and peaceful and you're paddling along a river, and then all hell breaks loose and you're forced to think and act fast. I love that part."

He unhooked his rope and sat down, too. "What about horseback riding?"

"That's one of those things I enjoy doing when I need time to think. I guess I find the cadence of the horse like a lullaby of sorts."

"What about when you're jumping over a fallen tree or a rock? Doesn't that kind of mess with the lullaby?"

She leaned against the upper step and closed her eyes. "Mess with? No, not really. Alter? Yeah, a little. You know how sometimes an exhausting activity can clear your mind of things that seemed such a big deal before you started? Well, working a horse hard does that for me. And the slow, wandering part gives me a chance to catch my breath and come up with a solution."

Mark's laugh brought her focus back on him. "So what you're telling me is that I need to learn how to ride a horse, huh?" Before she could respond, he moved the topic into a broader arena, desperate to keep the evening light and fun. "You ever think about changing the name of your company to Outdoor Therapy?"

"Sometimes the stuff on a person's bucket list is put there for therapeutic reasons." She swung her body to face him, hugging her knees to her chest. "But most of the time, learning how to ride a horse in adulthood, or rafting your way down a picturesque river, is about a dream. Sometimes it's a carryover from childhood— maybe from a television show or a book with a character who rafted or climbed or snorkeled. In those cases it's something my client has always wanted to do, and they're determined to do it before age makes it too difficult. But sometimes it's part of a broader dream that starts in a person's thirties or forties. Maybe they've always played life safe, or maybe they've been so busy caring for an elderly parent or a sickly kid that they need a diversion. Or maybe they're so intent on accomplishing some sort of personal feat that they show up at my door saying, *'I don't care what we do just so long as I can say I did something.'*"

"That happens?"

"All the time."

Mark considered her words and compared them to his own reasons for having enrolled in her orienteering class. His reasons, his motivations, put him in the latter group. "I guess I'm kinda like those folks. At least on some level."

"How so?" she asked.

"I think I needed to prove something to myself. Prove that I can change, can get myself out of a rut if I just make myself do it."

"And?"

"I did that," he replied. "Only now I want to see what other kinds of things I can do."

She released her legs and jumped to her feet, a sly smile tugging at her lips as she reached for his hand. "Okay, so let's see how you do with the intermediate wall."

He allowed her to guide him back there, only to wave off her attempts to hook him back up to the rope.

"Oh, come on, Mark, you can do this."

"And I'll give it a whirl in a few minutes. But first I want to see *you* climb."

"Why?"

He looked from the expert wall to the beginner's

and back again, finding the difference between the two substantial. "Because I want to see that someone can actually climb that thing."

Two minutes later, he was mentally patting himself on the back as he watched her climb the wall with the help of an electronic belay, the harness emphasizing her ass in a way that made him wish he was climbing right behind her, his body melding against hers as they moved from hold to hold.

Unfortunately, he wasn't in Emily's league, as evidenced by his repeated slips off the harder, more complex wall. But it didn't matter. He was having a blast nonetheless.

Here, the stress of day-to-day life was noticeably absent.

Here, he could laugh without guilt and live, rather than remember.

So he threw himself into the process of climbing, discovering what techniques worked for him. But even when he miscalculated, even when he out-and-out failed, it was still fun. Energizing, even.

Eventually, though, his arms and legs began to protest the workout, forcing him to unhook himself from the rope. "Emily? This was awesome! I don't know why I waited so long to try this kind of stuff. It's… *motivating.*"

She came down from yet another successful climb on the expert wall, and met him in the center of the room, her hand reaching for the straps of her harness, only to be shooed away by his.

"Please. Allow me." Snaking his arms around her midsection, Mark slowly unhooked them, the feel of her lower back beneath his fingertips making his shorts tighten in response. Carefully he set her harness on the floor, then pulled her close once again, the ache to kiss her stronger than ever before. But this time, instead of kissing her mouth, he drew his lips across her eyes, her cheeks, her chin, eventually sinking still lower, to the base of her neck.

When she laced her fingers in his hair, he moaned, her taste, her touch like some sort of magnetic pull he was powerless to fight. Seconds turned to minutes as his lips left her neck and traveled back up to her mouth, the warmth and yearning he found there making him moan again.

"Mark," she whispered against his mouth. "It's almost one in the morning."

"And your point?" he countered as his tongue slipped past her protests.

Bracing her hands against his chest, she stepped back. "Most people are heading to bed by now."

"Most people aren't standing in a room alone with *you,* Emily Todd." Her laugh caught him by surprise. "You think I'm kidding?"

When she didn't respond, he continued. "I can't tell you the last time I laughed as much as I have tonight. Or the last time I didn't want to escape into bed just to get the day over with. But tonight, with you, it's been different. Which means I now have a much better understanding of how much it stinks for Seth when I make him clean up his toys before he's ready to stop playing."

SHE MET HIM in the parking lot in the same outfit she'd worn when they arrived, the hint of appreciation on Mark's face worth the time it had taken to stop in her office and change again. "Everything's locked up, so we're good to go," she announced.

At the feel of his hand on hers, Emily looked up and smiled. "This was fun, Mark. It really was."

"Uh-oh."

She drew back. "Excuse me?"

"I said 'uh-oh.'"

"I got that. But why?"

"I was bracing myself for the big black moment."

She wiggled her hands free of his and rested them on her hips. "What are you talking about?"

"The black moment. You know, like that instant when you reach into your wallet to pay the toll and realize you're flat broke. Or when you've been craving some peace and quiet, only to get home and find that your water valve broke and your basement is flooded. Or better yet, that moment when you're standing at the baggage claim in your oldest pair of ripped blue jeans and you realize your suitcase is lost, and the meeting with your boss's boss regarding your long-awaited promotion is less than an hour away."

"Ooh-kay. So what black moment are you bracing for right now?"

He lifted his hand to her shoulder and then circled it around her neck, drawing her to him with a gentle force that nearly took her breath away. Slowly, deliberately, he brought his lips down on hers for what had to be the sweetest, most passionate kiss she'd ever had—the kind she wasn't likely to forget in this lifetime or the next. When he was done, he hooked his index finger beneath her chin and lifted her face just enough to leave a long, lingering kiss at her hairline, making her shiver in response.

"I'm bracing myself for the moment you say goodbye."

## Chapter Eight

Emily tried to make her laugh sound carefree, but it was obvious even to her that she'd failed miserably. She was falling for this man. To pretend otherwise required a kind of theatrical prowess she simply didn't possess.

"I don't want this to be a black moment," she finally whispered.

"Then say you'll follow me back to my house and come inside for a little while. Say you're not ready for our time together to end yet, either."

Startled, she glanced at the ground momentarily while she searched for something to say. All she came up with, though, was an echo of his words. "Your house?"

The lone light in the parking lot caught the concern on his face as he rushed to offer an explanation she wasn't entirely sure her body wanted to hear. "Oh. No. Not like that. It's just that I've really enjoyed hanging with you tonight, and I'm not too eager for reality to take over, you know?"

Problem was, she did know. She, too, found herself

in a world of married friends who were suddenly much harder to nail down for a movie or a coffee or even a walk in the park. She wasn't thrilled with the change, but she was used to it. Mark, however, probably wasn't. After all, his status as a single father was still fairly new.

"I could start a fire in the pit outside and we could sit on the patio and talk. Or if you'd rather, we could see if there are any good movies on cable. Whatever you want."

It took everything she could muster not to ask if he could kiss her again the way he had outside Kate's house, or even the way he had just now, on her forehead. Never in her history of kissing had such encounters zipped along virtually every nerve fiber in her body, waking up senses that had obviously been in a deep slumber for most, if not all, of her life.

Instead, she nodded, the answering smile on Mark's face one she wished she could bottle.

Reaching into her purse, she felt around for her keys and then headed to the driver's side of her car, the prospect of spending a few more hours with Mark intriguing. Once she was settled in her vehicle and he in his, he gave her the high sign from his window and motioned for her to follow him to the home he shared with his son.

When they arrived, she slid the Jeep into Park and looked to her right, absorbing the small white bungalow situated peacefully between two large oak trees. The front porch, while not terribly deep, welcomed with its whimsical summer flag and cozy wicker swing suspended on thick chains. The pathway that led to the steps boasted an assortment of black-eyed Susans, bee balms and even a few holdout blue flags.

His tap against her window prompted her to roll it down. "I see you garden?"

"Sally gardened. I'm just doing my best to keep everything—" his voice dipped ever so slightly "—*alive.* You know, so things look the same for Seth. He needs that sense of continuity and stability right now." Gesturing toward the walkway, Mark met her gaze through the open window. "Well? Shall we?"

"Um, sure." Squaring her shoulders, she stepped from the car and allowed him to place a guiding hand at her back.

Slowly, they made their way up the sidewalk and onto the porch, the answering silence of the crickets sending an unexpected shiver down her spine.

"Are you cold?" he asked, draping an arm over her shoulders.

"I think the more accurate word would be *nervous.*" The second the comment was out of her mouth, she regretted it.

"Hey." He turned to face her, the concern in his eyes impossible to miss. "There's no need to be nervous. This is just another setting for an evening that's been mighty special so far. That's it, okay?"

Two seconds later, as she stood in his front hallway, she knew Mark was right. The barbecue had given them a chance to size each other up. The time spent climbing had been about having fun and not worrying about Kate's prying eyes. And being here in Mark's house was just another opportunity to enjoy each other's company before their day-to-day lives took over.

Glancing about, she couldn't help but notice the homey touches that magnified the welcoming feel of the porch. Knickknacks and memorabilia dotted the shelves of a corner hutch off to her left, while a smattering of pictures lined the wall on her right, creating a sense of warmth and familiarity.

Emily approached the first picture, the image of a newborn Seth drawing her. "His hair back then was the same color as yours."

Mark's breath was warm on her neck as he, too, moved in closer. "It was. But it didn't stay that way for long. When he wasn't much more than five or six months old, the hair on the sides of his head started to disappear. Funny thing is, we never saw any clumps in his crib or on the floor. It just kind of disintegrated, replaced with the blond hair he has now."

"Your wife was blonde, I take it," Emily mused before stepping to the right to take in the next picture, of a slightly older Seth with a smile so big it transformed his penetrating blue eyes into a virtual carbon copy of Mark's. "Wow. He was every bit as adorable here as he is now."

And just like that, the same sparkle she saw inside the frame ignited in the eyes of the man who shadowed her footsteps. "He *is* a cutie, isn't he?"

"The cutest," she echoed. "But even more than that, he's sweet and kind and quite the little conversationalist. I've found myself actually missing him since the other night at Sam's."

Mark drew back. "You mean that was real the other night?"

"*Real?*" she parroted.

"Yeah. I mean, I kind of assumed you were just being nice and, you know, humoring him because he's four and still hurting over his mom."

She pulled her focus from the photograph and fixed it on the larger, dark-haired man beside her. "*You* don't humor him, do you?"

"No. But he's mine. It's only natural for me to think he's brilliant and funny and the best kid in the world."

Sinking against the wall, Emily did her best to explain the lift the little boy had given her by simply being himself. "Well, he's *not* mine. And as you know, I'd never laid eyes on him before that night. But it took all of about five minutes—which, for the record, happened sans you—for me to find him engaging, thoughtful and very sweet. It's like—" she looked past Mark as she searched for the right words among an unexpected minefield of emotion "—being around him erased reality for a little while and actually enabled me to step back into the part of the picture I *didn't* draw when I was ten, yet always knew was there."

"Wait." Mark held up his hand. "You mean the pictures in your office? I thought you drew them all. They certainly looked like they'd been drawn by the same—"

"There was one more. One you didn't see because I opted not to frame it, much to Kate's chagrin, I might add. But I'm talking about one I *thought* about drawing but didn't." Suddenly aware of how idiotic she must sound, Emily straightened and made her way to the next photo, farther down the hallway. It was of Seth at about two, his face not much different than it was now. "While I can't be sure how I would have drawn a little boy at that time, my dream son would have been everything I saw in Seth the other night. The same joy, the same curiosity, the same beautiful heart. And he would have been a spectacular big brother to the little girl I would have drawn in his arms."

"You were quite the little artist back then, weren't you?"

"No, I was quite the *dreamer.*"

"So you want kids? One boy, one girl?" Mark reached around her to straighten the frame, which had slipped off center by a fraction.

"I did. But I'm older now. Wiser, too." Feeling her mood begin to slip, she cast about for something to get things back on track. "Seth is just one of those kids who stick in your head and your heart long after they've run off, you know?"

At the feel of Mark's breath on her neck again, she turned to find his mouth settling on hers with an urgency that both stunned and excited her. Rising on tiptoe, she slipped her arms around his back and reveled in the feel of his strong, healthy body.

She gasped ever so slightly when he ran his fingers through her hair, pulling her head back so his lips could explore her chin, her jaw, the base of her throat. Her body responded with an undeniable warmth that left her heart pounding mere seconds before his hands started untying her halter top.

His gaze followed the straps as they cascaded down the front of her body to reveal even more of her breasts than her attire had already provided. Her breath hitched when his tongue slid over his lip in response.

"Emily?" he asked hungrily, before meeting her eyes and seeking permission to continue.

With a gentle yet deliberate finger, Mark lowered the fabric enough to reveal the lacy, strapless bra she'd bought during an extra girlie moment, his moan of desire instantly wiping away any regret she'd had over the price tag.

Slowly, deliberately, he moved his lips over the tops of her breasts, while his hands slipped behind her back and unfastened her bra. As the last hook was freed, the flimsy material fell away revealing the effects of his nearness. She cried out as his urgent mouth settled on her hardened nipples, teasing, caressing....

Suddenly he pulled back, desire blazing in his eyes. "Emily, I want you."

She answered by slipping her halter top the rest of the way off, her efforts rewarded by the appreciation in his eyes and the unmistakable bulge in his pants. Reaching around her waist, he undid the lone button on her waistband and watched her skirt fall into a puddle at her feet, revealing her white lacy thong.

"Oh my God, you are sexy as hell, Emily," he murmured against her ear. Grasping her hand, he led her through a small but tasteful family room and into a second, darker hallway beyond.

When they stepped inside his bedroom, he pulled her close, his fingers slipping around her waist, only to travel to her ass and tug her against his still-clad body, evoking a moan of her own.

He wanted *her*.

Emily.

MS and all…

RELEASING HIS HOLD on her, Mark stepped back long enough to take stock of the woman standing in the middle of his bedroom, his erection straining against the fabric of his shorts in response. Never in his wildest fantasies had he ever come across a female quite like Emily Todd.

Her eyes, her hair, her face spoke to his protective side, the innocence he found in her gripping his heart and threatening to never let it go. And her breasts spoke to him in a different way—tantalizing and teasing him with rock-hard nipples that confirmed his desire was reciprocated.

With determination befitting a Jedi warrior, he

forced his eyes from her breasts and allowed them to travel south, down her flat and sexy abdomen to the alluring scrap of fabric that separated him from a heat he craved as he'd never craved before. He sank to his knees and guided her panties down her legs with his mouth, letting the garment drop to her ankles so he could taste her sweetness.

Her answering moan of pleasure was followed by the feel of her fingers as they buried themselves in his hair. He wanted this woman. Wanted her now.

Rising to his feet, he steered her hands to the waistband of his shorts, watching her face as she released his erection with a tug. When she was done, he pulled her to him, the heat of their skin mingling as he laid her on the bed and lowered himself to her, their bodies joining effortlessly.

She felt so good and so right as he moved inside her—slowly and gently at first, then with gathering strength and desire. With thrust after thrust he claimed her, the intensity of his efforts making her cry out for more—a request he was all too happy to oblige, until neither one of them could resist any longer, their release coming so strong and so decisively it left his body craving an encore before the spinning in his head had even stopped.

# Chapter Nine

It was a full ten minutes or so before Mark opened his eyes, the fleeting confusion in his face at her empty spot in the bed giving way to a smile that warmed her the moment he spotted her standing in the bedroom doorway, wrapped in a bath towel, watching him.

The thin cotton sheet slipped from his chest as he rose on his elbow to give her a more thorough and appreciative once-over. "How long have you been standing there?"

She held her hand to the opening of her towel and picked her way across the clothes-littered floor, her other hand clutching the skirt and halter top she'd rescued from the hallway. "Not long. I—I took a shower in your guest bathroom. I hope that was okay. I got up about an hour ago and did some exercises that made me a little sweaty."

She could feel his gaze as she bent to retrieve her panties. "Exercises?"

"Uh-huh. Sit-ups, push-ups, that sort of thing."

"Naked?"

The huskiness of his voice warmed her face, rendering her unable to answer with anything more than a nod.

"Wow." He dropped onto his back and laced his fingers behind his head, a mischievous smile playing across his lips. "I'm getting worked up just thinking about that."

She glanced at the part of his body still covered by the sheet, the sudden elevation of the fabric just below his waist confirming his words. She swallowed.

Mark patted her side of the mattress. "Get back in here. I miss you."

"But my hair's all wet," she protested.

"Get back in here."

She set her recovered clothing on his dresser and made her way around the edge of the bed. "If you're sure."

He rose on his elbow a second time, the sheet slipping farther down his well-toned body. "Oh, I'm sure. Trust me. But lose the towel, okay?"

She paused, a sudden burst of self-consciousness making her apprehensive about granting his wish.

"Oh, no, don't go getting all shy on me now. Your body is exquisite."

Slowly, she peeled away the soft blue towel and slipped into bed beside him, where he coaxed her onto her side and pulled her back against his chest. She snuggled there, keenly aware of his still-hard length pressed to the base of her back. "It might not always be that way, you know," she murmured in a voice that was suddenly sleepy.

He kissed the top of her wet head a few times. "What?"

"My body. It could change in lots of ways."

The pressure of his lips ceased temporarily. "You've got a long way to go until you're old enough to worry about body changes. And even then, I suspect those worries will pass you by, with good reason."

She rolled over and planted a kiss on the tip of his chin. At his happy moan, she kissed him one more time and then looked up at the ceiling. "I'm not talking about age-related changes, silly. I'm talking about disease-related changes."

At his silence, she continued, transported back to countless nights and mornings over the past few months when this exact topic had played its way through her thoughts. With no one next to her to hear her fears.

"There are the obvious ones, of course, that most people think of when they hear the words multiple sclerosis. You know, wheelchairs, walkers, a funny lilt to your walk, that sort of thing. Then there's the chance that I could wake up one day and be temporarily blind, or unable to feel my legs or my arms or even both."

On a roll, she kept talking, the need to say everything out loud far stronger than she'd realized. "Sure, I know the meds I'm taking three times a week are designed to help stave off the disease as long as possible, and I'm grateful for them. But even those bring their fair share of issues. When I have to take a shot, I try to do it just before bed so I can sleep off the flulike effects. And if I don't get enough sleep on those nights, I pay for it with aches and pains in the morning. If I fail to take it before bedtime, as was the case last night, then I have to take it in the morning and basically deal with feeling lousy all day."

She drew a deep breath, letting it out slowly. "And then there's the bruising and stuff at the shot site." Shifting ever so slightly, she guided his gaze to the back of her arm, her abdomen, her hip and upper thigh, tapping a small red spot some eight inches above her knee. "You might not be able to see the marks a whole lot right now, unless I just took one, like I did before my shower. But over time, after months and years of injecting myself in the same places again and again? Well, they'll be impossible to miss regardless of how toned I might—"

A quick, yet persistent buzz cut her off midsentence.

Mark rolled to his left and reached toward the nightstand, retrieving his cell phone from beside the lamp. He looked at the display screen and sat up, flipping the phone open. "Good morning, little man. How'd you sleep?"

For the briefest of moments, Mark's lack of response to what Emily had shared stung ever so slightly. She'd kept everything to herself for so long it had felt good to know someone else was listening. To go from that to a phone call without so much as a squeeze or nod of acknowledgment was disconcerting.

Then again, he hadn't asked for the phone call to come at that exact moment, and it was Seth, after all. The same little boy who'd managed to grab hold of her heart with barely more than a smile. Yes, Seth Reynolds was a sweet boy, of that she was sure. She'd seen it in his devotion to his sand castle and the careful thought he'd given to the life he'd have inside its walls if he were truly a prince. She'd seen it in the way he'd listened so intently to his father's inquiries about her job and her clients while they ate, interjecting a few well-thought-out questions of his own on occasion. She'd seen it in the way he'd hopped down from his chair to retrieve a slip of paper a passing patron had dropped on the ground. She'd seen it in the way he'd shared tales about summer camp and his favorite times with Mark. And she'd seen it in his eyes when she'd first told Mark about her diagnosis.

Kids like Seth didn't become that way all by themselves. They were shown how by someone who was like that, too.

Stealing a glance in Mark's direction, she felt a warmth spread throughout her body that had absolutely nothing to do with physical desire and everything to do with genuine affection and admiration.

Maybe she really could frame that final drawing one day....

Maybe there really was a prince who could love his princess no matter what....

Content for the first time in a very long time, she

rolled onto her side and drifted off to sleep, the sound of Mark's voice as he spoke to his son the best lullaby and postinjection anti-ache ointment she could ever imagine.

"So TELL ME WHAT YOU DID with Gam last night. Did you get pizza?"

"Yupper doodle! And ice cream, too."

Mark closed his eyes at the happiness in his son's sweet voice, allowing it to soak into every pore of his being, and feeling his shoulders and neck muscles relax as it did. He was grateful for the result, but perplexed by the need.

He'd had an amazing time with Emily last night. She'd been both fun and funny at the barbecue, patient and encouraging on the climbing walls, and beyond his wildest expectations in his bed. They'd made love several times throughout the night, her enthusiasm and passion elevating the encounter into the best-ever category. And even when he'd awakened to find her watching him, he'd been happy. Truly happy.

Yet here he was, sitting inches from her sheet-covered body, and feeling the tension roll in all over again. It was subtle in nature, residing primarily in his upper body and temples, but it was present, nonetheless.

"And you wanna know what else we did, Daddy?"

Why on earth was he tense? It made no sense at all.

"Daddy?"

Mark shifted his focus from Emily to the dresser on the opposite wall. There, beside the pile of clothes she had placed on top, was the picture of Seth and Sally that greeted him each morning. It had been taken on their last outing together before the cancer had confined his wife to bed. Their smiles, so like one another's, still brought one to Mark's lips, too. Yet today, unlike all the other times he'd looked at that same picture and experienced the same reaction, the joy was fleeting.

Because there, on his son's face, was something he'd overlooked each of the other thousand or so times he'd stared at that photo.

Seth's mouth might have been smiling—a byproduct, no doubt, of having spent a special day with his beloved mom—but his eyes weren't. In them there was sadness—the kind of sadness only those who'd witnessed the suffering of a loved one could ever truly understand.

Mark swiped at the tears he felt forming, and willed himself to concentrate.

"Daddy? Are you still there?"

He tightened his jaw in determination. "I'm here, Seth."

*Focus...*

"Gam and me had *two* whole bowls of ice cream!"

There were so many things Mark wished he could go back and change from the moment Sally had received her diagnosis. Things about himself and the way he'd handled the situation that still haunted him six months after her passing. But of all the mistakes he'd made, all the regrets that had him pacing his bedroom at all hours of the night, the one he shed the most tears over was the one that concerned his son.

Or, rather, the way he'd let his son down during the most difficult time of the little boy's life.

"Did you hear me, Daddy?"

*Focus, damn it...*

"I'm sorry, little man. Can you say it again?"

"Gam and me had *two whole* bowls of ice cream! With whipped cream *and* candy pieces on top!"

"You mean one for her and one for you?" he asked.

"No! Two for each of us! And you know what else? Gam's new frigerfrator came and it was in a great big box!"

Mark resisted the urge to correct his son's pronunciation of refrigerator and addressed his enthusiasm, instead. "Sounds to me like you're more excited about the box than you are about her refrigerator."

"It's really, really big, Daddy. Bigger than me, and even bigger than *Gam* if she could stand up."

Closing his eyes, he imagined the smile that accompanied his son's words. He'd taken Seth's smiles for granted once. Now he knew better. "Wow. That must be a really big box."

"It is! And you know what? Gam said we can get out my crayons and turn it into a castle that I can actually go inside!"

Before Mark could weigh in, Seth chattered on. "And then guess what, Daddy? Guess what she told me?"

"What?"

"She said we can keep it in the playroom for as long as I want!"

He made a mental note to have some flowers on hand when his mother dropped Seth off that evening. Maybe even a box of candy, too.

"I love you, Seth," he whispered. "You know that, right?"

"Yupper doodle! And I love you, too, Daddy. Bunches and bunches and *bunches!*"

Long after his son had hung up, Mark held the phone to his ear, his focus trained on the photograph of Seth and Sally and the haunted look he was slowly but surely trying to eradicate from his son's deep blue eyes.

A warm hand on his bare back made him jump, and he snapped the phone closed.

"Everything okay with Seth?" Emily asked in a voice thick with sleep.

"Yeah." He propped his pillow against the headboard and reclined against it with a quiet sigh.

Emily rolled onto her side and smiled up at him. "So did he have some more pepperoni pizza?"

"Uh—what?"

Her smile faltered a smidge as he turned his head and met her gaze. "Seth. Did he have pizza last night?"

"I think so. I don't really remember."

Glancing back at the picture of Sally and Seth, he sighed again, this time more loudly and with a hint of impatience that made Emily sit up, his sheets drawn around her chest.

"Is there a problem with Seth?"

He looked from the image of Sally to the one of Seth in her arms, the hurt and loss of innocence in his son's eyes clawing at Mark's insides in a way he simply couldn't ignore.

And in that instant, he knew what had been nagging at his subconscious.

The tension he'd been feeling when Seth's call came in wasn't a coincidence. It was a warning bell. One he needed to heed before it was too late. He owed him that much.

Emily's hand closed on his and squeezed. "Mark? Is there a problem with Seth?"

"No." He cast about for the best way to remove the Band-Aid her presence had placed across his heart, and finally settled on the tried-and-true yank method that got it all over in one shot. "There's a problem with *us,* Emily."

"Us?" she echoed, all sleepiness slipping from her voice in favor of confusion. "I don't understand. What's wrong?"

He bit back the urge to halt the conversation and pull her into his arms before he ruined everything, because he had to say it. "I can't do this."

"Do what?"

He forced himself to meet her eyes. "This. You know, with us." He moved his hand back and forth between them. "Seth deserves...*better.*"

A wave of self-loathing washed over him as his

words hit their mark, but it was short-lived. His responsibility, his duty, was to Seth. It had to be.

"Better?" she echoed in confusion. "Mark, I don't understand what you're saying. Please tell me what's going on. Everything was fine five minutes ago."

"No. It wasn't."

"Yes, it was. And you know that as well as I do."

He had to make her understand. "I have to make a better choice for Seth. It's my job."

"A better choice?" she whispered through suddenly clenched teeth. "Wait a minute. I get this now. This isn't about finding someone better. It's about finding someone healthy, isn't it? Someone who doesn't have to take shots, or have bruises all over her body? Someone who won't slow you down or embarrass you because she slurs her speech in front of your friends."

When he didn't respond, she scooted to the edge of the bed and traded the sheet for the towel she'd shed on the floor. With three easy strides, she crossed the room and pulled the pile of clothes off his dresser.

He fought back tears as he watched her march toward the door, the sight of her retreating back making it hard to breathe. But he had to let her go. He really had no choice. His life choices weren't about him. Not anymore.

Yet as she reached the doorway, he couldn't help but call her back one more time. For one more glimpse at the ray of sunshine that had graced his life and his bed for one amazing evening he knew he'd never forget.

"Emily?"

Without turning to look at him, she paused there.

"Please know that the Folks Helping Folks Foundation is here to help you in whatever way you need as this disease progresses. It's what we do, and we're really very good at it. And the Longfeld donation I told you about yesterday? That could really help you in ways you may not even be able to realize yet." He could hear his voice growing hoarser with each passing word, the overwhelming sadness at losing this woman making it difficult to speak. "So, please, give it some thought. If you decide to come on board and let us help, I'll assign Bob to your case—he's the best. He'd take good care of anyone, but if I give him a heads-up that I know you, he'll take even better care of you. I promise."

Slowly she turned, her clothes clutched against her body with trembling hands. "Let me make this crystal clear to you, Mark. I don't want or need Bob's help and I most certainly don't want or need yours, either. I am fine, and I will continue to be fine. On my own. The way it's supposed to be."

He opened his mouth to protest, but shut it as she continued, her voice, her demeanor, taking on an icy quality.

"And just in case it's unclear, being on my own is the way I *want* it to be."

# Chapter Ten

Emily pulled into the parking lot beside Perk It Up and cut the engine, the only tangible remnant of her morning a dull ache above her eyes that more than served her right. She'd been a fool giving Mark a second thought, and an even bigger one for giving him a chance at her heart.

But it wouldn't happen again, that was for sure.

Leaning forward, she peered into the rearview mirror for any sign of the tears that had birthed the headache, aware of the trouble she'd be in if Kate suspected she'd been crying. Then again, she could always pin her red-rimmed eyes on the aches and pains that had racked her body all morning long.

A rap on her driver's side window made her jump.

"Would you stop checking yourself out in that mirror and get moving, already? I'm in desperate need of my jumbo size mocha latte. *Now.*"

With a quick swipe of her hand through her hair, Emily grabbed her purse from the passenger seat, mustered the best smile she could and met Kate on the walkway that led to their favorite coffee shop. "Long morning?" she joked as they headed inside for their weekly get-together that had been a tradition since they graduated from college.

"Long night, long morning, take your pick. It's all kind of blending together at this point." Kate swept her hand toward the seating area. "Why don't you get us a table and I'll get our drinks. That way there won't be an issue finding a table. You want your usual?"

Emily considered saying no and asking for a simple glass of water, but knew it was best just to nod. Any deviation from normal where Kate was concerned was too risky. Especially today, when Emily was one funny look away from screaming at the top of her lungs until the men in white suits arrived to cart her off to some padded room somewhere.

No, her best chance of getting through the next hour was to act as normal as possible and keep control of the conversation, steering it toward innocuous subjects like work, Kate's favorite reality show, Joe and the status of Kate's baby-making quest.

Selecting a table beside the large plate-glass window, Emily peered out at the comings and goings of downtown Winoka. Everywhere she looked there were couples—teenage couples, young married couples, elderly couples, and everything in between. It was as if the only way people got from point A to point B in this town was by holding hands and stopping every few feet to make googly eyes at one another.

It was maddening, really. A little nauseating, even.

"You do realize I've been climbing the walls ever since you left the barbecue last night, don't you? I think I checked my cell phone close to a hundred times before Joe finally hid it in his den somewhere." Kate paused beside Emily's chair and studied the bold black initials snaking their way down the seam of both foam cups. "Okay, here you go, this one is yours."

Claiming the empty lattice-back stool across from her, Kate perched on the edge and widened her eyes, waiting. "Well? What do you have to say?"

Emily looked from her to her coffee cup and back again. "Oh, yeah. Sorry." With an appropriately timed cringe, she remembered her manners. "Thanks for the coffee, Kate. I'll pick them up next week, okay?"

Her friend shook her head and laughed. "Nice try."

Slowly she lifted her cup to her mouth and took a sip, Kate's gaze never leaving her face. "What? What am I failing to say?"

A squeal from her friend took her and the rest of the patrons in the coffee house by surprise. "I want to hear everything. And by everything, I mean *everything*. Don't leave anything out. Not one single, solitary thing."

"That last sentence was rather redundant, don't you think?" Emily set her cup back on the table and wrapped her hands around it. "But really, Kate, I have no idea what you're talking about."

Pushing her own cup to the side, She leaned in. "You know, I told Joe you were going to do this. In fact, I think I nailed your line almost verbatim." A pause for reflection gave way to a slow, yet self-satisfied nod. "Actually, you know what? There's no *almost* about it. I got every last word with the exact same inflection and everything. Wow. I've really got you down, don't I?"

"Kate. Would you knock it off, please? I have absolutely no earthly idea what you're babbling—"

And then she knew.

There would be no time-killing conversation about her upcoming fall classes, no stories starring Joe as the perfect husband, no idle chitchat about the latest fashion trends being worn about town that day. And there would be no graphic details about Kate's ovulation cycle or the number of times the happy couple did it during the primo thirty-six hour target that month.

No, the conversation had already been picked out for them hours earlier, when she'd made the mistake of bringing a male guest to Kate and Joe's barbecue....

"You do realize I could sit here and give you all sorts of grief over you having gone out to dinner with this guy and his son *days ago* and never saying a word, but I won't. I could also give you all sorts of grief over your failure to call and fill me in on everything when you got home last night, but I won't. Part of being a good friend is patience and understanding, right? Which, technically, I gave you by not bugging you for details until now." Kate grabbed her cup and took a big sip, fanning her mouth as she did. "Ow. Hot."

"There's nothing to tell, Kate."

"You have pizza with a super hot guy, bring him along to my barbecue and then forget to call me with all the deets afterward, and you expect me to believe there's nothing to tell? Are you nuts?"

Pushing away the image of Mark's bare chest as it rose and fell above her body countless times throughout the night, Emily addressed her friend's inquiry as quickly and succinctly as possible. "Look, I saw him and his son at the beach when I was kayaking. I let him take Seth out in the kayak for a few minutes, and they tipped over. Seth was fine because he had on Floaties, but I swam in and got him nonetheless. To thank me, they took me out for pizza. No big deal."

"Most no-big-deals don't look at a woman the way yours looked at you last night," Kate said.

Emily lifted her cup, only to set it back down as her hands began to tremble ever so slightly. "I don't know what you're talking about. Mark wasn't looking at me in any special way last night."

"Oh, no? Then I guess every single one of my friends who commented to me about the two of you last night was imagining the same thing I was?"

"And what was that?" she asked, exasperated.

"That your no-big-deal is more than a little hot for you."

Hot for her.

She couldn't help it—she laughed. It was either that or cry. And she knew if she opted for the latter, she wouldn't be able to stop anytime soon. "I think you *and* your friends all need your eyes checked."

Kate took another sip. "It sounds to me like you're the one who needs your eyes checked. I mean, c'mon, Em. That guy couldn't keep his eyes off you. And when you talked…either to him or with one of us? He *listened*. And I mean, really listened. As if the words coming out of your mouth were the most fascinating things he'd ever heard." Kate eyed her across the lid of her cup. "Are you really going to sit there and tell me you weren't aware of that?"

Emily pulled her hands from around her own drink and dropped them into her lap. She'd revisited Kate's barbecue innumerable times that morning, reliving many of the things her friend was spouting. Of course she'd seen the looks Mark had sent in her direction. Of course she'd been aware of the way he listened when she spoke. And yes, she remembered every single minute of their time together. But none of that erased the cold hard facts.

Kate released a long, dreamy sigh through pursed lips. "I mean, Emily…really. Mark turned heads last night. Happily married heads, I might add. And it wasn't just because he's good-looking. A lot of it was because of how attentive he was to you." A quick laugh gave way to a faraway look. "He was gentle and kind and funny, and so helpful with everything where you were concerned."

Emily glanced up. "Helpful?"

"He carried your plate out to the Adirondack chairs, didn't he? He opened the door for you every time you went in the house, and picked up your horseshoes after every round you played."

Before she could fully process everything Kate was saying, her friend continued on in a voice that had suddenly grown more hushed. "He really seemed to care about you, Em. Like he'd do just about anything you needed him to do, if you'd only *let* him."

Instantly, she remembered being in his arms, the sensation of his hands on her face so strong in her mind that she could actually feel them.

"I mean, you're so wrapped up in this stupid nightmare you keep having about being a burden that you're missing the possibility of what could very well be right in front of your face. In an extremely attractive package, I might add."

"Stupid nightmare?" Emily echoed.

"Yes. A stupid nightmare. I mean, come on, Em. Don't you realize how silly it is to let some recurring dream keep you from the one thing you've wanted since we were little?"

"I wanted lots of things when we were little," she reminded Kate before slipping off her stool and tossing her nearly full cup into a nearby trash can. "And I'm living them right now."

"Not all of them."

"I'm living the ones I have control over."

Kate grabbed Emily's hands and held them tight.

"No man who has a clue what you're worth would ever shy away from you because of the MS. It just wouldn't happen."

She clenched her teeth and muttered, "Oh? You don't think so?"

"Of course I don't. Joe doesn't, either. You just need to let the right guy see the true you—without that silly nightmare clouding the picture. The rest will fall into place. We're sure of it."

Emily weighed her response as she gathered her purse in her hands and hooked it over her shoulder, her desire to hide her hurt superceded by a need to make things clear. "Then perhaps it's not your eyesight that needs to be checked, but rather, your intuition. And if you have Joe's checked, too, maybe you can get a discount. You know, a check-one-check-the-second-for-free kind of thing."

It was Kate's turn to protest. "Why are you being so negative? This isn't like you."

Closing her eyes, she counted to ten, praying for patience and something resembling civility.

"Are you going to let your diagnosis make you shut down Bucket List 101?" Kate challenged.

Emily opened her eyes as she hit five. "Of course not. You know better than that."

"Then why would you let it keep you from finding someone special? That makes absolutely no sense to me, Em!"

"Then let me spell it out for you, Kate. Living my dream with Bucket List 101 affects me and me only."

"That's not true. What about Trish?"

Emily rolled her eyes. "Trish is nineteen. She'll be married in a few years. And once she and Tommy have kids, she won't be working anymore. But if I build a life with another person, this illness will affect him at some point, too. *That* isn't fair."

"And you think a guy like Mark couldn't handle your MS?"

"I don't *think,* Kate. I *know.*" She saw the way her friend jumped back at the anger in her voice, but she couldn't help it. She'd had enough. Her head had come out of the clouds the second the neurologist had walked into her hospital room and uttered her diagnosis six months earlier. It was time for Kate's head to come out of the clouds now, too. "So Mr. No-Big-Deal can find someone else to open doors for, and carry plates for, and pretend to listen to as if she's the only woman on the face of the earth."

Emily's breath hitched as the tears she'd vowed she wouldn't cry in front of her friend began to form in the corners of her eyes. "I just hope, for her sake, she has a super strong immune system, capable of withstanding the common cold and flu. Because if she doesn't, she'll surely be getting the Mark Reynolds seal of disapproval where it comes to him and his son."

Kate's gasp netted more than a few curious looks in their direction. "Emily! You can't truly believe that."

"Oh, no? Hmm. Do you know why I didn't call you last night when I got home from your barbecue?"

"No…"

"Well, here are some deets for you, Kate. I didn't phone because I didn't go home after the barbecue."

Emily lowered her voice, abruptly aware of the hush at several neighboring tables. "I took Mark to the office and taught him how to climb. We laughed, we joked, we had a great time. And then, when we were done climbing, I went home with him…and we slept together. When we woke up, I shared a few of my realities with him, only to have him essentially toss me out of his bed *and* his life. So don't you dare sit there and tell me I can't believe what I just said, because I can and I do."

Stopping for a much-needed breath, she steadied her voice and her emotions until she could finally escape to the privacy of her car. "But no worries, Kate, I'm fine. I'd much rather live my life in a way that fits *me*. Besides, for what it's worth, the days of wanting that fairy tale prince—from that silly picture I drew at your kitchen table a lifetime ago—to sweep me off my feet are long gone. And you know what? I'm okay with that. A-okay, as a matter of fact."

A flash of pain skittered across Kate's face. "But—"

"Because when it comes right down to it, I'd much rather walk on my own two feet than count on anyone else, anyway. It's the surest way I know to get where I'm going, don't you think?"

## Chapter Eleven

Mark made his way through the house, turning on lights and fluffing throw pillows as he went, his ear turned toward the driveway for the sound of his mother's car. For far too long, he'd sat in the gathering dusk replaying his time with Emily—remembering every smile and every laugh they'd shared.

Desperate for something to deaden the ache in his chest, he strode into the kitchen and over to the refrigerator, liberating a rare can of beer from the top shelf and popping the tab. Try as he might, he couldn't get the image of her beautifully toned and naked body out of his thoughts.

One-night stands had never been his thing, even during his pre-Sally days. And last night, when he'd made love to Emily, that hadn't changed. What, exactly, he'd thought they had or could have, he wasn't sure, but he knew he'd wanted to see her again.

Yet all that had changed the moment he'd heard Seth's voice juxtaposed against the last photograph he'd taken of Sally and Seth together.

It didn't matter what he thought of Emily. It didn't matter how alive she made him feel or how perfect it felt to be inside her. He wasn't a single man. He was a single father. There was a big difference between the two.

"Daddy?"

He placed his beer can on top of the refrigerator and met his son in the hallway, squatting down and holding out his arms. "Little man! You sure are a good tiptoer. I didn't even hear you come in."

Seth stopped just shy of Mark's arms. "I didn't use my tippy toes, Daddy. I even banged the door, but you were making that silly face."

Dropping his arms, he studied his son closely. "Silly face? What silly face?"

"This one." Seth leaned against the wall, opened his mouth a little and stared off into space, before breaking the pose with a giggle. "See?"

Mark had to laugh. "Oh, sorry. Daddies get distracted, I guess." Then, opening his arms once again, he greeted his son in the way he'd intended before letting his thoughts stray to a topic best left in the shadows. "Do you have any idea how glad I am to see you, little man?"

It was true. Seth was the glue that kept his life together, the reason he got up every morning and came home from work every evening. Without him, Mark would be lost, his life empty of any real purpose.

Seth squeezed him with all his might, a curious

aroma of Play-Doh and chocolate chip cookies clinging to his hair. "Gam wants you to wave before she leaves."

Lifting his son into his arms, Mark made his way to the front door and blew his mom a kiss before locking up for the evening. "So did you make your castle with Gam out of that great big box you told me about when you called?"

Seth nodded. "I did! And it is so-o-o neat, Daddy. Gam said I could show it to you next week when I'm back in camp and you have to pick me up at her house after work."

"I can't wait to see it." He carried his son into the living room and set him down on the couch, claiming the cushion to Seth's left. "Maybe, if I can find another box, we can add on an addition. Like a throne room or something."

His son's eyes brightened with genuine excitement. "I bet my princess would like a special room for all her fancy dresses."

"Your princess, eh? Is she pretty?" Mark teased, ruffling Seth's hair with his fingers.

"Yupper doodle. The prettiest."

He considered the little boy's words with all the seriousness he could muster, and consciously relaxed his shoulders. "That's quite a claim, little man. Tell me about her."

Tucking his legs beneath him, Seth took a deep breath, releasing it along with a lengthy description. "She's got great big brown eyes that twinkle with so much pixie dust that some of it falls over the top of her nose and across her happy cheeks. She's got short yellow hair that curls right here—" he pointed at the sides of his face "—and a really big smile all the time."

"Wow. She *does* sound pretty. Special, too. Just like you." Mark pulled the little boy's head onto his lap. "I missed you last night and this morning. I didn't have anyone to make my special pancakes for."

Seth giggled. "You could make me some tomorrow morning."

"Yes, I can."

"So what did *you* do, Daddy?"

"I ate cereal."

Seth's giggle grew louder. "No, silly. What did you do last night while I was at Gam's?"

Mark forced a smile and did his best to keep his voice light. "I played some horseshoes."

"Is that a game?"

"Yes, it is." He tapped Seth's nose with his finger and animated his voice. "You use real horseshoes, just like the kind real horses wear on their feet."

"Where'd you play with those kinda shoes, Daddy?"

"At a barbecue I went to."

"Whose barbecue?"

"No one you've ever met."

Seth sat up, eyes wide. "You went to a stranger's house, Daddy? You know you're not s'posed to do that. It could be dangerous."

He tried not to laugh at his son's solemn expression.

"Well, they weren't strangers, exactly. The people having the barbecue are friends of the person I went with."

"Who'd you go with?"

He exhaled into the palm of his hand, his discomfort over the shift in topic increasing exponentially. "I went with Emily."

"Emily!" Seth parroted, just before a smile spread his lips wide. "Oh, wow, I like Emily. Bunches and bunches!"

Clapping his hands together, Mark seized on the only sure-fire conversation changer he could find. "You know what I found in the cabinet earlier today?"

Seth shook his head.

"Butterscotch sauce and a bag of mini chocolate chips. And I figured, if you're up for it, maybe we could make our own ice cream sundaes right here at home," he said in his best conspiratorial voice. "So what do you say, little man? Does that sound like a yummy plan for after dinner?"

"I already had dinner. At Gam's. She made me eat all my broccoli." Seth looked toward the door and lowered his voice to a near whisper. "It wasn't very good."

"But it's good for you." Mark scooted to the edge of the couch and glanced back at him. "Come on. Let's have a treat."

"Did you find whipped cream, too? 'Cause sundaes are s'posed to have whipped cream, Daddy."

Grateful for his son's one-track mind where ice cream was concerned, Mark rose to his feet and motioned for him to follow. "As a matter of fact, I did. A great big tub of it."

When they reached the kitchen, Seth climbed onto his stool at the counter and Mark grabbed a pair of bowls from the cabinet, along with two spoons from the utensil drawer. Then, with as much pomp and circumstance as he could muster, he set about getting everything they would need for their sundae bar, including the jar of sprinkles Seth spied while Mark was extracting the chocolate chips from the pantry.

"Do you think Emily likes ice cream, Daddy?"

He paused with his hand on the freezer door, his back to his son. "I can't answer that, Seth." Reaching inside, he pulled out two cartons and held them up. "So what'll it be? Vanilla or chocolate? Or—" he winked "—a little bit of *both?*"

"I betcha she likes vanilla best, just like me," Seth declared.

Mark's shoulders drooped. So much for changing the subject.

He carried the cartons to the counter and set them beside the bowls. "Maybe. I don't know." Then, with the help of the old spoon-under-warm-water trick he'd learned from Sally, he scooped two small mounds for Seth and two for himself. "Mmm. Finding that butterscotch sauce today was a pretty nice surprise, wasn't it?"

Seth propped one elbow on the counter and reached

for the sauce with his other hand. "Can I put it on all by myself, Daddy? Please?"

*If it'll make you forget about Emily...*

Aloud, he said, "If you're really, really careful, sure. But let's try to make that bottle last for a while, okay? That way we can have sundaes again another day."

"Okay! Maybe Emily can have some then, too, right?" Seth pulled the lid off the butterscotch sauce and carefully tilted it in the air above his bowl. Slowly, carefully, he poured some across the top of his ice cream, and then did the same to Mark's. When he was done, he turned the container upright and smiled. "See? I saved plenty for Emily."

Not wanting to stomp all over his son's mood, Mark made a show of adding a dollop of whipped cream to both bowls and then allowing Seth to decorate them with a few tiny handfuls of chocolate chips and a quick shake of the sprinkle jar. Once the last chip was placed on each sundae, Mark declared their concoctions ready to eat.

"Now, what do you say we try and see which one of us can eat all our ice cream from start to finish without making a peep? Whoever wins gets to pick which story we read before bed."

"Can I say it's yummy if it's yummy?" Seth asked.

"No, sirree. No yummies, no lip smacking of any kind, and—" he sat on the stool next to Seth and touched his finger to the little boy's nose "—most especially, no burping."

A fit of giggles gave way to the quietest ice cream eating Mark could ever remember, and he was glad. Whatever it took to keep Seth from talking about Emily. Mark's feelings for her were still way too close to the surface.

All day long he'd revisited moments from the barbecue, his favorites revolving around the game of horseshoes he'd failed at again and again. She'd been so good-natured and easygoing that she'd coaxed the same qualities out of him despite his lack of prowess or points. And when they'd gone climbing inside her office building, she'd made him feel as if there wasn't anything he couldn't do.

But it was the part that came later—in his bed—that he'd found himself lingering on. Every touch, every sound, every move was replayed in his thoughts until he'd had to force himself to focus on something else.

Now that Seth's chattering had ceased, though, Mark found himself pressing the play button in his mind once again. And sure enough, an image of Emily looking up at him as he made love to her flashed before his eyes, making him drop his spoon into his bowl with a metallic crash.

"Daddy, you made a noise!" Seth accused. "A great big loud one!"

Shaking away the memory, he turned to the towhead sitting beside him. "So I did."

"I won! I won!" Seth jumped off his stool and headed

down the hallway to his bedroom. "And I know exactly the story I want to read. It's my very, very favorite!"

Thirty minutes later, once Seth had had a bath and brushed his teeth, Mark settled atop his son's covers with the selected book—a story about a young prince and princess and their fairy-tale castle in an enchanted forest. Mark tried hard to make the story come alive by calling on his best repertoire of voices for all the main characters. The effort delighted his son.

When they reached the end, Mark closed the book and laid it on the night table. "I think that's my favorite story, too."

"Daddy?"

He looked down at his son and smiled. "Yes, little man?"

Seth let out a big yawn. "When can we see Emily again?"

Closing his eyes, Mark searched for yet another way to change the subject—something he could say to end their evening on a happy note instead of one tinged with guilt and the kind of highlight reel that was sure to haunt him as he slept. Yet all he could come up with was a truth Seth needed to hear, if for no other reason than Mark's own sanity. "Son, I'm afraid we won't be seeing Emily anymore."

Seth's eyes widened with questions Mark was simply too tired and too strung out to answer. Instead, he swung his legs over the edge of the bed and made his way to the door, stepping out into the hallway and flipping off the overhead light as he did. "Good night, little man. Sweet dreams. I'll see you in the morning."

SETH STARED UP AT THE sliver of light the moon cast on his ceiling, and wiped the wetness from his cheeks. The lump in his throat kept getting bigger and bigger no matter how hard he tried to swallow it away.

He was trying to be brave, like a big boy, but it was hard. God kept taking all the happy, smiley princesses for himself.

Like Mommy.

And now Emily, too.

Rolling onto his side, Seth pulled his stuffed giraffe, Geronimo, against his damp cheek and stared out the window into the night, the sadness on his daddy's face when he'd told him about Emily making the tears come faster.

He remembered Emily saying she was sick, but he hadn't known she was going to leave so fast. And once again, just like with Mommy, he hadn't gotten to say goodbye.

Daddy had. Daddy got to hold Mommy's hand when she went to be with God. But *he* was too little. He'd had to stay with Gam.

Daddy got to go to a barbecue with Emily and see her smiles one last time. But *he* didn't. He was having two whole bowls of ice cream with Gam.

Why didn't anyone ever let him say goodbye? Didn't his goodbyes matter, too?

Sitting up, he looked into the giraffe's black shiny eyes. "I want to say goodbye, too, Geronimo. Don't you think Emily wished I could say goodbye just like Daddy got to?"

He nodded the animal's long neck in agreement.

"Yeah. Me, too, Geronimo."

His mind made up, Seth slipped from his bed and tiptoed over to the closet for his quietest pair of sneakers and his favorite backpack. Then, being extra quiet, he put his softest baby blanket and his special picture of Mommy inside the main pocket and zipped it up tight, his uneaten Pop-Tart from yesterday still packed safely in a side compartment.

Careful not to make any noise, he made his way across his room to his bedroom door, which Daddy always left partway open. With a quick left and a right, Seth headed over to the sliding glass door in the living room and stopped. Then, peeking over his shoulder toward his daddy's room, he pushed the little silver lever into the unlock position. When he was sure Daddy hadn't heard the click, he stepped outside and slid the door shut.

"C'mon, Geronimo," he whispered as he crept around the house and onto the street, his feet taking him in the same direction Daddy's car always went. "It's our turn to say goodbye."

## Chapter Twelve

Emily propped her elbows on her desk and stuck her fingers in her ears in a futile effort to drown out the steady *whump whump* of the helicopter flying back and forth over Bucket List 101.

She tried to concentrate on the course description she was composing for the upcoming fall calendar, but the incessant noise made writing difficult at best. No matter how many times she consulted the list of skills her students would learn during the four-day extreme camping expedition, she forgot them the second she began typing, her thoughts, derailed by the persistent feeling that something wasn't right...

She knew it was silly, paranoid even. It was a helicopter, that was all. Its very nature was to push down air, thus putting pressure on a person's eardrums. Pulling her fingers from her ears, Emily rose from her chair and made her way to the window, the maddening *whump whump* of yet another pass overriding her need for fresh air.

"Hey there, boss." Trish breezed into the room, her

slim legs making short work of crossing to the desk. "I compiled a list of twenty former clients who expressed an interest in a survival-style camping trip when they filled out their comment cards at the end of class. Gives us a nice solid base to start with, don't you think?"

Emily turned away from the window. "That sounds like a great idea. Nice work, Trish."

She rounded her desk and dropped back into her chair, repositioning her hands atop the keyboard. "Now, if Mr. Helicopter Instructor would just take his student a few miles east, I might actually get the darn course description written and ready for you to paste into the fall program guide."

Trish strode over to the window and peered out. "That's not a flying lesson, boss. It's a search team."

"Search team?"

"Uh-huh. According to my mom, they're looking for some little kid who was missing from his bed this morning."

Emily's stomach tightened with fear at the mere notion of what that would be like for a parent. "Boy or girl?"

"A little boy."

"How old?" she asked.

"I think my mom said he's four, maybe five, but I'm not exactly sure. I *do* know he's not school-aged yet."

Jumping up, Emily joined Trish at the window. "Call the local police station. See if they'll fax you some information on this little boy. If they can do that, tell them

I'm willing to call in some of our more seasoned hikers and see if we can get together a search team to go out into the woods on foot."

Ten minutes later, Trish was back, fax in one hand, pink sticky note in the other. "Got the info you requested, boss. A picture, too."

"Tell me."

Consulting the note, Trish began filling in the blanks. "Okay, the kid's name is Seth Reynolds and—"

Emily's gasp echoed against the walls, only to be drowned out by an eighth helicopter pass and Trish's voice relating, "He's four and—"

"A half," Emily cried. "Four and a half. Oh my God, Trish, I know him."

Her assistant's eyes widened. "You do?"

She reached out, grabbed the fax from her hand and stared down at the face of the little boy who'd smiled so sweetly at her across the dinner table at Sam's. "This is Mark's son."

"Mark?"

"Yes. You remember Mark."

Trish looked questioningly at her. "I do?"

"He's the guy who came to my orienteering class late the other day! The one who…" She let the words trail off. There wasn't any other meaningful correlation to be made for Trish or anyone else. Not now. Not ever.

Looking back down at the paper in her hand, Emily read the word for word quote Mark had given the police department's dispatcher: "My son isn't the type to wander off, but he's been through a lot lately, losing his mom and all. I mean, I thought he was doing okay—as okay as he can be, anyway, but maybe I was wrong. Maybe I missed something. But he's a sweet little guy who loves his toys and dreaming about fairy tales and castles."

"Dreaming about fairy tales," she whispered. Suddenly she was back on the beach at Lake Winoka. Seth's sand castle was to her left, while Seth himself played in the sand, wide-eyed and happy. In her hand was the flag she'd crafted out of a stick and a leaf. She was glued to the spot by Seth's tales of royalty and secret hideaways....

"Secret hideaways," she whispered, before grabbing Trish by the arm. "Oh my gosh, Trish, that's it! *That's it!*" She released her assistant's arm, only to grab for her purse and keys. "I've gotta go. Cancel my class for this morning and the one this afternoon, too. Tell people we'll reschedule for next week—same day, same time. If they can't make it, give them a refund."

DESPITE THE TEARS that had clouded her vision on the drive home from Mark's twenty-four hours earlier, Emily was able to find her way through downtown Winoka and out the other side with little to no effort, her hands instinctively turning the wheel down one side street after another until she was back on Crystal View Drive. Any hesitation she entertained as to which house was the right one was quickly wiped away by the smattering of police cars parked outside the fourth bungalow on the left.

She pulled alongside the curb behind the last of four Winoka police cruisers and cut the engine, her heart thudding in her chest. All the way there she'd second-guessed her decision to come, her worry over getting Mark's hopes up unnecessarily almost making her turn around. But every time she slowed the car to do just that, Seth's voice had gotten louder in her head.

If she was wrong, she was wrong. But if she was right, and she did nothing…

Dropping her keys into her purse, she stepped from the car and crossed the street to Mark's house, a huddle of police officers quickly disbanding as she approached. "Can I help you, miss?" one asked her, not unkindly.

"I'm a friend of Mark's. I'd like to see him if it's okay."

The officer hesitated a split second before waving her through. "Yeah, okay. But he's in bad shape right now. Might be helpful if you can get the poor guy to eat something. He's gonna need his strength if this drags on."

She nodded and continued up the driveway, her feet guiding her to a door she'd vowed she would never step foot in again. But this was different. Her being here had nothing to do with her and nothing to do with Mark.

This visit was about Seth and only Seth.

When she reached the front porch she knocked,

only to be instructed to enter by the same police officer who'd given her permission to pass.

Was she crazy for being here? For pretending she actually knew Seth in a way that made her privy to his thoughts?

Maybe.

But it was worth the shot. *Seth* was worth the shot, she reminded herself.

This time, when she entered Mark's home, she didn't linger in the hallway looking at pictures. She knew they were there, knew Seth's eyes were on her as she nodded toward the officer standing there and turned her focus to the living room and the man with the chocolate-brown hair who sat slumped in a chair, staring at the carpet beneath his feet.

She hesitated, for a moment, his private pain slowly thawing the anger she held for him. She couldn't imagine what he was going through—the raw fear he must feel, wondering if he'd ever seen his precious little boy again.

But before she could muster the courage to speak, before she could settle on just the right sentiment to offer, a board creaked under her feet. At the sound, Mark's head snapped up and his eyes widened. "Emily?" he choked out. "What are you doing here?"

Pushing aside all residual anger for the man, she crossed the room and stood awkwardly beside his chair. "I heard about Seth."

Mark's head pitched forward once again, his shoulders caving inward. "He was in his bed when I went to sleep last night. I kissed his head and tucked him in bed with Geronimo. And then…this morning…he was *gone*. They both were."

Gathering her courage along with her breath, Emily put words to the scenario that had played itself out in her thoughts again and again throughout the drive. "Did you check his tree house?"

Mark's head moved from side to side. "Seth doesn't have a tree house."

"Yes, he does," she said. "He told me all about it at the beach the other day."

In a flash Mark's eyes were on hers, penetrating, questioning. "What are you talking about? What tree house? Seth *doesn't* have a tree house."

Slowly she lowered herself onto the couch across from Mark and reached for his hand, the feel of his skin against hers and the subsequent thumping in her heart something she'd have to chastise herself for later, when she was alone. "The other day, at the beach, before you came over…Seth and I talked about the castle he was making and which room he'd live in if it was real."

Mark's eyes closed and he gave a tired shrug. "Seth is big on fairy tales. Has been ever since he was old enough to sit on Sally's lap at bedtime and follow along with the pictures in a book while she read the story aloud. Something about her voice when she read the princess stories left an impression on him. By the time he was two, those had become his favorite, and that hasn't changed."

Emily shook his hand ever so gently until his focus was on her once again. "Please, Mark. I need to tell you this. After he showed me his room in the castle, I told him that I used to dream about living in a castle when I was little, too."

"Emily, I don't see why any of this matters. My son is *missing!* Don't you get that?" Pulling his hand from hers, he raked it through his hair. "He could be wandering around lost, or be with someone who intends to do him harm."

She continued on, undaunted. "I told him that just because my dream didn't come true, there was no reason to think his couldn't…because dreams are good and special, and no one can ever take them away from us unless we give up on them ourselves."

Sensing Mark's growing frustration, she plowed on, desperate for him to see the tree house tidbit the way she did—as a viable place for finding Seth. "That's when he told me about his tree house. He said he found it in the woods."

Mark straightened in his chair. "Woods? What woods?"

"I'm not sure, exactly. I think he called it Gem's Woods or something like that," she recalled, unsure of whether she was saying the right name. "I suppose it could be a place in his imagination, but he talked about it like it was real. Like it's a place he's gone before."

"Say the name of the woods again," he prompted.

"Gem...Gum...Gam... Something close to—"

He drew back. "Did you say Gam?"

"That's the closest I can remember. I'm sorry...."

"No. No. Don't be. That's what he calls my mom. It's a carryover from when he had a hard time saying his *r*s when he was first learning how to talk."

"Are there woods behind your mother's house?" Emily asked.

"There are, but her house is easily a mile away from here. He couldn't walk that by himself. He's only four."

She nodded, even as she relayed the rest of the conversation she'd had with Seth. "He told me he liked to climb the ladder and sit there. He said he liked to go there and dream with his eyes open."

"Dream with his eyes open?" Mark repeated in confusion.

"He said that he likes to dream that way best because then they're not as scary as the ones he has at night in his bed."

This time, Mark brought both hands to his face and peered at Emily across the tips of his fingers, clearly trying to absorb everything she was saying. After a few seconds, he jumped to his feet so forcefully his chair tipped over backward. "Oh my God, do you think that's where he went?"

She rose in turn, finding the hope on Mark's face both encouraging and frightening at the same time. "I don't know. I really don't. But if there's even a tiny chance that's where he went, it's worth trying to find it, don't you think?"

"Absolutely!" he shouted as he ran toward the door, with Emily at his heels. "Anything is worth a shot at this point!"

## Chapter Thirteen

The police car had barely come to a stop in his mother's driveway before Mark was out of the front seat and opening the back door for Emily. "Come on, let's go! Hurry!"

Together, they took off in a sprint around the neatly kept house where Mark's mother lived, and headed into the woods, their path slowed from time to time by a downed tree and the occasional large rock that posed a tripping hazard to anyone not paying attention. With unspoken agreement, they split off in opposite directions when the trail they were following did the same, one branch leading toward a rushing creek, the other farther into the woods.

Emily turned left and darted around an old rusty fence that marked some long-ago property line at the base of a steep hill. Without breaking stride, she ran to the very top, her gaze flitting from side to side for any indication of the tree house Seth had spoken about that day at the beach.

He hadn't given her anything to go on, no concrete

description of the path he took to get there that could now serve as a map. What she did know was that the tree house had a long ladder, which meant the structure was elevated a fair distance. From the perspective of a four-year-old, anyway.

Running through the woods was something she was good at. Emily could weave her way around trees and toppled limbs like a football player tasked with the job of getting the ball down the field and into the end zone. But that was when she was looking straight ahead, not up, as was currently the case.

Everything she knew about missing children pointed to the importance of time. The longer a family went without finding their child, the less likely they ever would. So the urgency to locate Seth's tree house and rule it out as a possibility was critical. With that in mind, she lowered her head and began searching for the ladder rather than the tree house itself, enabling her to run faster.

And that's when she saw it—a rotting, weathered affair that looked as if it could barely support the weight of a curious squirrel, let alone a human. But Seth was light and compact.

Without altering her stride, Emily stuck her fingers in her mouth and gave a long, low whistle to alert Mark to her find. The ladder she'd spied grew closer and closer, until she could just make out the bottom of an old tree house that had clearly seen better days. When she reached the actual tree, she said a silent prayer, hoping against hope that her gut was right—that Seth was inside, dreaming, safe and sound and completely oblivious to the massive search now under way in his honor.

With barely a pause to collect her breath, she began climbing, the second board of the makeshift ladder giving way beneath her feet and prompting her to grab hold of the fifth board and pull herself upward. Two more big pulls and she was emerging through the floorboards into a dank and dusty place that smelled vaguely of strawberry Pop-Tart. Squinting into the darkness, she choked back a sob of relief at the sight of the little boy and his stuffed giraffe sleeping peacefully beneath a blue-and-white baby blanket, a framed photograph of Mark's late wife peeking out from under the soft fleece.

Slowly but surely, a parade of tears made its way down Emily's cheeks. "Seth? Seth, wake up, sweetie. It's me, Emily. From the beach and the pizza parlor the other night."

"Emily?" the little boy repeated in a voice heavy with sleep. Slowly, he sat up, furiously rubbing his eyes, then peered at her between the ears of his giraffe. "Emily? Is that really you?"

She heard the crunch of leaves on the ground below as Mark reached the tree, prompting her to move away from the hole in the floor to afford him access to his son. "Yes, Seth, it's really me."

"But how did you come back?" he asked, his eyes round with confusion.

"Come back?" she echoed. "Come back from where?"

"From God's house!"

She moved aside as Mark pulled himself into the tree house and lunged across the floor, drawing his son into the fiercest bear hug she'd ever seen. "Seth… Seth…*Seth!* You scared me half to death! What were you *thinking* by leaving the house like that in the middle of the night?"

The little boy pointed over his father's shoulder. "Daddy, look! It's Emily! She came back from dying!"

She looked from Seth to Mark and back again, the child's bizarre statement throwing her for a loop. "Dying? Seth, I didn't die. I'm right here, perfectly fine as always. See?"

Wiggling out of his dad's arms, Seth turned a questioning eye on Mark. "Daddy, you told me we wouldn't be seeing Emily anymore, remember? You told me that last night, when you were kissing me and Geronimo good-night."

Mark's mouth gaped. "Is that why you ran away, little man? Because you thought I meant that Emily had died?"

Seth nodded solemnly. "I didn't get to say goodbye. So I came here…to say goodbye in my wake-time dreams. Just like I did when Mommy died."

"Oh, little man, come here." As he gathered his son in his arms once again, Mark's shoulders began to shake, an indication of the tears Emily suspected were streaming down his face and onto Seth's head.

Mark was right.

Seth cared about her way too much. Especially for someone so young, who had been through so much already. He'd grieved enough for one lifetime.

Swallowing painfully, she made her way back across the floorboards to the ladder. She'd done what she'd set out to do. She'd found Seth and reunited him with his dad. It was time to go home.

SECONDS TURNED TO MINUTES and minutes to half an hour as Mark sat there in the tree house, holding his son close, grateful for the chance he'd been so sure he'd lost.

When he was convinced the moment was real rather than a cruel dream from which he'd soon waken, he brushed a hand across his eyes and released Seth for a long-overdue once-over. "Do you have any idea how worried I was when I woke up this morning and you weren't in your bed? Or how scared I was that someone had gotten into the house and taken you? Or that I'd never get to hold you in my arms again?"

Seth's cheeks turned crimson and he cast his eyes downward. "I'm sorry, Daddy. I didn't mean to scare you."

"I was afraid you were all alone and waiting for me to find you." He heard the words as they left his mouth, the fear, relief and anger in his tone shaking him to the core once again. Now that Seth was safe, Mark realized just how terrified he'd been while he'd sat waiting for some word. It was a feeling he wouldn't wish on his worst enemy.

Seth raised his stuffed giraffe in the air and waved it around for Mark to see. "I wasn't alone, Daddy. Geronimo was here to keep me safe. Mommy, too."

"M-Mommy?" he sputtered.

"I talk to Mommy here. And she listens to me."

Mark sucked in a breath as he searched for the right words. Clearly, it was time to bring in a professional— someone who was trained to help his son through his grief. Raking his hands through his hair, Mark asked, "What do you say to Mommy when you're here?"

Seth rocked back on his knees, and smiled. "The first time, when I just found my tree house, I got to tell her goodbye. And then I made sure to tell her that I love her very, very, very, very, very much. Because she needed to know that, Daddy. She really did."

"Mommy knew how much you loved her, little man. It's why she smiled like she did all the time." Shifting slightly, Mark reached for Seth once again, this time pulling him onto his lap. "There wasn't a day that went by when Mommy didn't know how much you loved her and how very special she was to you. And you know what? That was the greatest gift you could have ever given her."

"But I wanted to tell her goodbye *before* she went with God. Just like you got to, Daddy. Only you and Gam didn't let me. You said I was too little. But little people can say goodbye just as good as big people. Geronimo thinks so, too."

Mark considered his son's words and compared them

with the decision he'd made as Sally's death neared by hours rather than days. "I'm sorry you didn't get to say goodbye to her, Seth. I really am. It's just that…well, all I can say is that sometimes big people have to make a decision they think is right. And I thought it was more important for you to remember Mommy the way she was the day before she died—when you were able to cuddle up next to her, looking through the pages of your favorite storybook together." He heard his voice give way under the weight of the memory, and he worked to compose himself so he could say what needed to be said. "I didn't want your last memory of Mommy to be one where she could no longer say anything to you. Because that's what it was like for me, and it was really sad."

Seth nestled against Mark's chest, his hand wrapped tightly around Geronimo. "It's okay now, Daddy. I said goodbye to Mommy in my wake-time dreams. And she heard me, because she made a rainbow right out there—" he lifted his giraffe and pointed it toward the square opening that served as the tree house's lone window "—as soon as I told her. It was big and had lots and lots of pretty colors. Even purple!"

Mark wanted to ask about the rainbow, but opted to leave the topic alone. If Seth needed to see a rainbow to make peace with his mom's death, then he needed to see a rainbow. Telling him that such a sighting in thick woods was nearly impossible served no real purpose.

Sometimes being right didn't matter. And this was one of those times.

Instead, he lifted his hand to Seth's head and smoothed back the crop of blond hair that was so like Sally's. "How did you find this tree house? Because I know you couldn't have gotten Gam out here all by yourself."

"I found it the day Mommy died."

"I get that," he said. "But how did you find it?"

Seth shrugged. "I found it all by myself."

He swallowed. "Gam let you go out in the woods by yourself?"

"No. Gam didn't know. She was crying in her room. But I knew why. I knew God had given Mommy her wings so she could fly like the rest of his angels. 'Cept she's extra special because she's a princess angel."

Mark gave the nod he knew Seth needed, but stuck to his line of questioning. "So how did you end up all the way out here? By yourself?"

"Gam fell asleep. She didn't mean to, Daddy, but sometimes crying makes you sleepy. So I asked Geronimo if he wanted to help me find the hospital, and he said he did. But we found this tree house instead. When Mommy made the rainbow, we went back and woke up Gam."

Mark shook his head at his lapse in parenting. His own pain had been so raw when Sally passed that he hadn't thought to go home for Seth until his own tears were in check. "Did you tell Gam about the rainbow?"

Seth grew quiet on his lap.

"Seth?" he repeated. "Did you tell Gam about the rainbow?"

This time, his son shook his head and whispered, "No."

"Why not?" he asked.

"Because the rainbow was *my* goodbye, Daddy."

Seth's goodbye.

A goodbye that could have proved disastrous if Emily hadn't remembered Seth's mention of a tree house.

"Emily," he mumbled under his breath, before glancing toward the ladder for the first time since finding Seth. "Where'd she go?"

"She climbed back down the ladder a long time ago, Daddy. Right after she winked a big wink at me."

"Why didn't you say anything?"

"Because you were crying, Daddy. And Emily put her finger to her mouth, like it was a secret."

"I was crying because I thought I'd lost you." Leaning his head against the wall of the tree house, Mark thought back over everything he'd heard. "And I can't ever lose you, little man. I love you too much for that, okay?"

"Okay, Daddy." Seth gestured around the tree house. "So do you like it?"

He let his eyes follow the path indicated, and nodded. "Did you at least tell Gam about the tree house?"

Again Seth shook his head. "Gam wouldn't like the ladder. She'd tell me I'm too little to climb it. Then all my dream time would be the scary nighttime kind again."

Opting to bypass the notion of nightmares temporarily, Mark asked the one question that still remained. "Seth? If you didn't want to tell Gam or me about the rainbow or this tree house, what made you tell Emily about it that day at the beach?"

"Because she wanted to live in a castle when she was little, just like me, Daddy. And just like Mommy did."

His breath hitched. "Your mommy wanted to live in a castle when she was little?"

"Uh-huh. And she got to!"

Mark smiled despite the tears that pricked his eyes once again. "She did?"

"Yupper doodle. And she lived in it with you and me, Daddy. She told me her castle was our house."

"She did?" he asked, blinking rapidly.

"Uh-huh. Every night when she kissed me and Geronimo good-night!"

It took everything Mark had not to break into wrenching sobs, the sadness he felt nothing short of overwhelming. "I'm sorry, little man. I'm sorry you had to lose Mommy when you're still so little."

With a lopsided shrug, Seth tossed his beloved animal into the air and caught him with a giggle. "That's okay, Daddy. It was better to have a special mommy for a little while than no special mommy at all."

## Chapter Fourteen

Emily pulled into the parking lot of Bucket List 101, her thoughts running in a million different directions, yet converging all in one spot. Seth was safe and sound, and that was all that truly mattered.

It was time to put the rest of the story behind her, where it belonged. Her passion was her company. She needed to focus on making it the premier outdoor adventure destination in the region.

No, she didn't have a husband and the prospect of children to look forward to, like Kate. But she had a company that was changing lives. Was one really better or more important than the other?

With a quick shake of her head, Emily grabbed her purse from the passenger seat and her keys from the ignition and headed toward the large white barn she'd converted into her offices, on the western edge of town. Here, she could be herself—adventurous, free-spirited and healthy. At least as far as her clients were concerned.

She pulled the door open and stepped inside to find

the reception desk empty. "Trish? I'm back. You still here?"

The soft squeaking sounds of her assistant's shoes preceded her appearance in the outer office. "My mom just called. She said the good news is all over the television and radio stations."

Emily felt the smile spread across her face. "We found him. Sleeping peacefully inside an old tree house in the woods behind his grandmother's place, completely oblivious to the search taking place all over Winoka."

"Is that why you went tearing out of here this morning?" Trish asked, claiming her spot behind the desk.

"I'm sorry about that, Trish. I really am. But all of a sudden I remembered something Mark's—*Mr. Reynolds's*—son had told me when I saw them at the beach after work the other night. He'd mentioned a tree house he'd found, and that he liked to go there to be by himself."

"Be by himself? Why does a four-year-old need to be by himself?"

Emily placed her purse on the floor, and perched on the edge of the desk. "Well, considering this particular four-year-old lost his mom to cancer six months ago, I imagine he's probably got more reasons than either of us could fathom."

Trish tsked softly. "Wow. That's rough. Thank God you found him, though." Reaching into her top drawer, she pulled out a couple of apples and offered one to Emily.

"Oh, thanks, I missed lunch." She reached for the fruit and took a bite, her mind wandering back through the morning, but stopping short of the many reasons seeing Mark had been so hard.

"Wow. So that guy—the one who was in here for the orienteering class? He lost his wife and then he couldn't find his son? Wow." Trish narrowed her eyes in thought as she crunched her own apple. "I think if I were that kid's dad, I'd be tempted to stick him in a bubble where he couldn't ever get lost, or sick, or whatever."

Pulling the apple from her mouth, Emily tossed the barely eaten fruit into the trash and stood, her appetite suddenly squashed. "No. Mark's preferred bubble isn't one that keeps Seth *in,* it's one that keeps everyone else *out.* Of Seth's life."

She heard the bitterness in her voice, felt the weight of Trish's questioning eyes and literally grasped for the first topic she could find to change the subject. Her hand closed over the first in a long line of pink sticky notes attached to her assistant's desk. "I take it I missed a few calls while I was out? Anything important or truly exciting?"

Trish glanced downward, running her fingernail along the line of messages. "I signed up this person… and this person…and this one, all for next week's Intro to Nature's Workout Room and…oh, yeah, this woman—" she peeled off the fourth note and gave it a quick glance before handing it to Emily "—is from *Winoka Magazine*. She wants to do an article on you."

Taking in the reporter's name and information, Emily nodded. "You mean an article on the company, right?"

"No. On you. She says she'll touch on the company in the story, but this particular piece is on female entrepreneurs and the spark that lit their proverbial match, as she put it."

"My proverbial match, eh? Hmm. Something tells me a little kid with a big imagination and a sixty-four pack of crayons probably isn't the kind of tale she's looking for."

"I'd read it," Trish quipped, moving her finger to the next note and pausing.

"Yeah, I guess I'd read it, too. And I'd probably send a copy to my mom for her scrapbook. So I guess we'd have three readers, if nothing else."

"Boss?"

At the change in Trish's tone of voice, Emily glanced up from the notes in her own hand. "Yes?"

"There was one other call. From a man named Jed Walker."

"And?"

"He started out as a prospective client at first, but then…"

She looked from Trish to the note in question and back again. "But then what? Is there a problem I should know about?"

Her assistant peeled the note from her desk and

crumpled it in her hand, shrugging as she did so. "Nothing we can really do anything about. But I still felt bad."

"Bad about what?"

"Not being able to help this guy. I mean, he knows he can't go wheeling through the woods with a compass or whatever, but it's kind of a shame that he can't take one of your survival seminars simply because he can't get down the stairs and into the classroom, you know?"

Finally, Emily was able to make sense of what she was hearing. "Is this guy disabled or something?"

"He's in a wheelchair. Lives on his own. He's got this dream of learning how to scuba dive one day despite the fact that he's paralyzed, and he was hoping he could sign up for one of your scuba trips to the Caribbean this winter. I told him that wasn't possible, but that we might be able to get some people in here to carry him in and out of the classroom if he wanted to sit in on one of your survival classes, but he said no. Said he gets where he needs to go on his own, without anyone carrying him around like a baby." Trish tossed the paper wad into the trash beside her desk. "The guy was a real firecracker, I tell you. Real determined to live life on his own terms, just like you. When I mentioned the survival class idea, he said it wouldn't do him much good anyway, since most campgrounds have gravel parking lots and are situated much too far from the actual facilities.

"Made me kind of sad when he said that. I guess I'm so used to being able to walk that I never really stopped to notice how life isn't set up for people like Mr. Walker."

Emily peeked into the trash can. "And this guy wants to learn how to scuba dive, when he can't walk?"

Trish nodded. "Said it was his dream long before the car accident that confined him to his wheelchair—"

The ringing of the office phone cut their conversation short, sending Trish into full-blown assistant mode and Emily down the hall toward her office, the image of the wadded-up pink sticky note front and center in her thoughts.

She understood all about determination. It was why she was standing in the middle of a building she'd purchased with the intention of starting her own company. A company that was now thriving, thanks to her own refusal to give up.

She understood the desire to live life on one's own terms. It was why she wouldn't let Kate cajole her into a life she was no longer meant to have.

And she understood the man's refusal to let people carry him around. The mere thought of being in that position one day with her multiple sclerosis was enough to drive her batty.

So how could she continue to tout Bucket List 101 as a way to fulfill lifelong dreams if she wasn't equipped to do that for everyone—especially someone as driven and full of heart as the man whose name was scrawled across a piece of paper now crumpled in Trish's trash can?

Deflated, Emily reached inside her office door and flipped on the overhead light, her gaze going to her desk and the pamphlets Mark had left behind prior to the barbecue and a night she wished she could forget, but knew she never would.

She'd been so angry when he'd brought the literature by, so quick to tell him she didn't need any help from him or his foundation. But now, in light of the man Trish had had to turn away because they were unable to accommodate his challenges, maybe it was time to rethink that notion.

When she was sure her assistant was off the phone, she pressed the intercom button. "Trish?"

"Yeah, boss?"

"We're about helping people realize their dreams, aren't we?"

"That's what the little thingy out here in the waiting room says."

"That's what it says in here on my desk, too." Leaning forward, she poked a finger at the replica of the sign that greeted her customers from atop a table in plain sight of Trish's desk. "Which means we've got a whole bunch of work to do to make that happen."

"Isn't that what we're already doing, with the course descriptions and the classes we keep adding?"

"But we can do better. We can do more. If we don't, we'll need to take down the sign we're both looking at right now." She swiveled her chair to the right and flipped on her computer, ready to begin the initial legwork for something she should have done a long time ago. "Oh, and Trish? When you get a chance, would you bring that message in here?"

A pause gave way to a funny little snort. "Uh, boss? I already gave you all your messages."

"I'm talking about the one in your trash can...the one with Mr. Walker's phone number on it. There are some things I'd like to discuss with him."

MARK PULLED HIS CELL PHONE from the side pocket in his car door and scrolled through his recent calls, finding the number for Bucket List 101 among them. He found it hard to believe it had been only five days since he'd first laid eyes on Emily. So much had happened.

She'd affected him in a way he hadn't seen coming. Sure, he wished things were different, that they could have met twenty years in the future, when he didn't have to worry about Seth quite so much. But they hadn't and he did.

His son had to come first.

*Seth.*

Leaving him with Gram for a much needed nap had been difficult. But the only reason Mark had been able to tuck Seth in for a nap at all was because of Emily. The least he could do was say thank-you.

Unfortunately, it was all the other things Mark wanted to say and do to her that kept pushing their way into his thoughts and leaving him more than a little unsettled. He wanted to shower her face with kisses of gratitude. He wanted to run his hands down her exquisite body. He wanted to peel off her clothes and make love to her all over again.

But he couldn't.

She was sick. And he was a father.

His mind made up, he pressed the button for Emily's office number and put the Blue Tooth device to his ear, the clamminess of his hand a shameful reminder of why he was suddenly so nervous. If a friend had led on a woman the way he'd led Emily on the other night, Mark would have been disgusted.

And he was. At himself.

Emily deserved an apology as much as she deserved a thank-you, and he would make sure she got both by the time their call was over. As he listened to the phone ring, he prepared himself for what to say and how to say it. But when it became apparent no one was going to pick up, his nerves gave way to disappointment.

What was with him? Wny couldn't he just shut this girl out?

A sixth ring yielded to a seventh before the call was finally answered. "Bucket List 101, this is Trish, how can I help you?"

He steered his car around a parked car at the end of his mom's road and stopped, his uncertainty over what to say rivaled only by his uncertainty over where, exactly, he was going in the first place.

"Hello? Is anyone there?"

*Say something, idiot...*

"Uh…yeah, hi. This is Mark. Mark Reynolds. I took a class on orienteering from your company the other day and I—"

"Mark, hi. Wow. I couldn't believe it when Emily told me the missing boy was yours. I bet you haven't let him out of your sight since she found him in that tree house for you."

He closed his eyes momentarily, the image of his son alive and well in the corner of the dilapidated tree house bringing a tightness to his throat. It was all still so surreal. "You have no idea, Trish. No idea."

She paused, then said, "I bet you want to talk to Emily and say thanks, huh?"

Among other things, he thought. To Trish, he said, "I do. Can you put me through to her?"

"Emily is out of the office at the moment. And since she didn't tell me where she was going, I can't be sure when she'll be back—if she even comes back this afternoon at all. But I can certainly put you through to her voice mail, if you'd like."

It wasn't the way he wanted to do it, but maybe it was for the best. That way he could thank her for finding Seth, apologize for his own shortcomings and then leave her to her life. "Yeah, okay, that'll work."

But the second he heard Emily's voice in his ear, he knew he couldn't leave a message. Calling her wasn't just about saying thanks. Or even apologizing. He wanted to hear her voice—talking specifically to him. He wanted to look into her eyes, wanted to scale a mountain with her by his side, wanted to learn about her past. He wanted to tell her one of Seth's jokes and hear the way she laughed with her whole being. Heck, he just wanted to be close to her again....

No. A voice message was not the way to tell her how he felt, or to explain why he couldn't see her again.

Ending the call, he turned left at the next cross street, his destination suddenly clear.

## Chapter Fifteen

Mark paused, his fist inches from the door, and turned toward the telltale sounds of a garden hose being used somewhere off to his left. Sure enough, in a quick peek around the corner of the house, he spied the very woman he was there to see, quietly humming to herself as she watered the same flowers and bushes he'd admired two days earlier. Without a moment's hesitation, he retraced his steps to the sidewalk and then cut across the side lawn.

Kate's cat-green eyes widened in surprise as she released her hand from the hose's trigger. "Mark? What are you doing here?"

"Hi, Kate. I was hoping you'd remember me." He held out his hand in her direction and was aware of the hesitation that accompanied hers in return. "I was wondering if we could talk. About Emily."

"What about her?" Kate squeezed the trigger once again and aimed the water across a row of zinnias.

He followed the stream with his eyes and searched for the best way to explain the jumbled mess in his head and why it had brought him to Kate's door. But before he could start, she'd moved on to the marigolds and her own assessment of him. "You know, I thought you were a nice guy the other night. So did my husband and the rest of our friends. In fact, if you want to know the truth, I kept Joe up for hours that night, going on and on about how perfect you were for Emily."

A flick of Kate's wrist brought the water dangerously close to Mark, yet he resisted the urge to flinch. She was angry, of that there was no doubt.

"But boy, was I wrong," she hissed. "In fact, I'd go so far as to say that it's guys like you who give the entire male gender a bad rap."

"I like her, Kate. I like her a lot." He linked his hands behind his head, only to release them just as quickly. "Do you think I'd be here, subjecting myself to the possible drenching that's mere centimeters—and quite likely *seconds*—away if I didn't?"

The spray of water came even closer. "Candy and flowers, or even—get this—*a date,* are generally the preferred ways to show a woman you like her, Mark. Telling her you're not interested because she has a life-altering condition doesn't really have the same ring, you know?"

He pushed his fingers through his hair and tugged, the frustration coursing through his body almost enough to make him pull it all out by the roots. "And if I handed my four-year-old son a toy truck and told him to take it out onto the middle of Highway W and play with it there, would you think I was a horrible parent?"

Kate turned the hose back on the zinnias, but kept her anger focused squarely on Mark. "Oh, are you one of those analogy guys? The kind who are always looking for some stupid little anecdote to justify their pathetic selfishness?"

His head was beginning to spin. "No. I'm just a dad who loves his son more than himself."

Rolling her eyes, Kate released the trigger. "What on earth are you babbling about?"

With the threat of a drenching removed, he gestured toward the corner of the patio. "Can we sit out back and talk? Please?"

For a moment, he thought she was going to refuse, maybe even turn the hose back on and actually point it at him this time. But in the end she nodded, lowering her arms with reluctance. "You've got five minutes. So you'd better get to the point. If you actually have one, that is."

Oh, he had one all right. Even if he wasn't entirely sure what it was yet.

He followed her through the break in the dwarf bush honeysuckle hedge and onto the patio. Once she'd claimed a spot on a cushioned chaise, he settled on a nearby Adirondack chair. "I don't know how much Emily told you about me, but I have a son, Seth. He's four and a half. In fact, if you watched the news at all today, you probably saw him on television."

"I didn't. I slept in and then I had an appointment."

"Anyway, his mother—my wife—passed away six months ago after a yearlong battle with cancer. It would have been a tough go for any kid to lose his mom, but Seth's anguish was magnified tenfold by my selfishnes."

Looking down at the stone slabs beneath his feet, Mark continued. "You see, I shut down. I couldn't stand watching her deteriorate, knowing there wasn't a thing I could do to stop it. I couldn't fight it away with my fists, I couldn't hug it away with my arms and I couldn't cajole it away with my words. I was utterly helpless and, well, I guess you can say I don't do helpless all that well. Or, as was the case with Sally's illness, at all."

At Kate's silence, he stole a glance in her direction, finding the blatant irritation that had all but seeped from her pores earlier suddenly gone. Temporarily, at least.

Not wanting to miss the opportunity her change in mood offered, he went on. "So while I buried myself in my work during her struggle, my three-and-a-half-year-old son was everything I should have been. He was her arms, he was her ears, he was her comfort and her companion. Which means he *watched* her die, Kate." His voice breaking, Mark dug his elbows into his thighs and cradled his head with his hands. "I failed her. And I failed my son. That's a mistake I'll have to live with for the rest of my life."

The creak of Kate's chaise was followed by a warm and steadying hand on his shoulder. "There isn't a rule book for something like that, Mark. You didn't know."

He snapped his head up, the pain in his voice replaced by the intense anger he felt for himself. "While I think that's a piss-poor excuse for my actions, I could only use it once. If I failed him like that again, I'd be the worst father on the face of the earth."

"Failed him again?" Kate asked, her eyes locked on his. "I don't understand what you mean."

"There was nothing I could do about Sally getting sick. It just happened. I should have been there for her, as a husband is supposed to be, and I should have been there for Seth, too. But I wasn't. And as a result, my innocent little boy saw far more of his mother's suffering than he should have. Losing his mom at that age was horrific enough. Having to experience that and play the part of the adult in the house at the same time? There are no words for that except *inexcusable* and *pathetic*."

At her obvious confusion, he filled in the blanks as succinctly as possible. "I cannot sit back and allow my son to love a woman I already know to be sick. It's like telling him to take that toy truck I mentioned earlier and play with it the middle of a four-lane highway. It would be certain disaster."

Kate's gasp brought him up short. "Wait. You don't think Emily is going to *die,* do you? Because she's not."

For the briefest of seconds he felt a hint of hope, only to have it disappear just as quickly. "Look, I'll be the first to admit I don't know that much about multiple sclerosis, but I know it can be extremely debilitating over time."

"That's true."

"I don't want Seth to have to watch someone he loves suffer ever again."

"And if you get sick, Mark? What then? Are you going to abandon him on the steps of some church, just so he doesn't have to watch you die? Do you really think that would be better?"

He pushed himself from the chair and paced across the patio, the thought of Seth being left orphaned one he hadn't visited before. "That falls into the category of things I can't really control, beyond doing my best to eat right and exercise more. But there's a big difference between something that's out of my control and something in my control."

Kate perched on the edge of the chair Mark had vacated, and exhaled. "Oh. I get it now. If you let Seth get attached to Emily and she suddenly starts going downhill, you've essentially handed his heart over to be broken once again."

Mark stopped midstep, deflated. "Yeah."

"Have you seen Emily? Have you seen the kind of shape she's in?"

In the interest of avoiding saying anything that might get him slapped, he opted to nod rather than put his feelings about Emily's body into words.

"You've got to know she's not going down without a fight." Kate stood and made her way over to him, a genuine smile on her face now. "Couple that with the fact that the medication she just started taking is designed to hold this thing at bay for a long time and, well, I don't think your reason for denying yourself a second chance is all that valid. Especially since it would be a second chance for Seth, too. A second chance to love and to be loved."

A second chance.

Was that what he wanted?

Mark wasn't sure.

And what about Emily? Was she even interested in a relationship? He posed the question to Kate.

"Oh, to hear her talk? No. But like you, Em has let the fear of what-ifs in life keep her from her dreams."

He had to laugh. "Are you kidding me? From what I've seen, Emily is all about chasing down her dreams."

"That's true for all but one of them."

"Huh?"

Wrapping her hand around his, Kate pulled him toward the back door. "Come. I want to show you something."

Five minutes later, standing in her sunny kitchen, he found himself staring down at a child's drawing. The blonde figure depicted on the page seemed vaguely familiar. "Is this one of Emily's?"

"Yep."

He couldn't help but smile as he took in the glittery crown on the subject's head and the huge smile on her face as a brown-haired boy, also wearing a crown, carried her into a castle in his arms. "She dreamed of being a princess?" he finally asked.

"She dreamed of finding her prince." Sweeping her hand toward the drawing, Kate dropped her voice to a near whisper. "It's the one dream that's yet to come true. Though if you ask me, it's closer than she realizes."

He took in the innocence and hope that had belonged to a ten-year-old Emily, and then handed the picture back to Kate. "So what's holding her back from making that dream come true, like all the others?"

Kate looked from Mark to the picture and back again before depositing it in his hands again with purpose. "She's afraid she'll be a burden to her prince because of her diagnosis."

"That's ridiculous," he argued. "You love the person, not the illness."

"You love the person, not the illness," Kate echoed. "Hmm… I couldn't have said that any better if I tried."

As heavy as his heart had been when he pulled into Kate's driveway, the opposite was true on the way out. Mark really didn't know if it was a second chance he wanted or not. He was okay raising Seth on his own. He was okay filling his days with work, volunteering at the foundation and being a dad to the greatest kid on earth.

But whether it was about second chances or something entirely different, he knew he wanted Emily. He wanted the lift she brought to his heart. He wanted the hope she sprinkled around with the mere flash of her smile. He wanted the contentment he felt with her in his arms. And he wanted the pure joy he saw in Seth's face whenever he was around her.

The ring of his cell phone broke through his thoughts. Seeing the name and number of the foundation's president, Stan Wiley, on his caller ID screen, he answered. "Good afternoon, Stan. What can I do for you?"

"I saw you on the news just now. So glad you found your boy safe and sound."

Mark smiled. "Yeah. You and me both." He pulled to the side of whatever street he'd gotten himself onto. "I'm not even going to ask how I looked. I barely remember talking into the microphone outside my mom's house."

"You looked fine. Rattled, sure. Relieved, absolutely. But no worse for the wear."

"Good." He made a mental note to call his mom the second he and Stan were done talking, to give her a heads-up on his estimated return and to hear Seth's voice. "So what can I do for you?"

"You can pat yourself on the back, Mark, for a job well done."

"I wish I could take credit for finding Seth, but I can't. That was a woman named—"

"No. No. I'm talking about getting us that Longfeld donation. Your hard work is going to end up benefitting a lot of people, Mark. A *lot* of people."

"You mean we got the donation?"

"You bet we did. And it's because of your hard work."

"*My* hard work?" he echoed. "Stan, I'm not sure what you're talking—"

"Of course, there's still work to be done, but that's usually the case with any accomplishment in life."

Mark tried to make sense of the conversation, his confusion growing with each word Stan uttered.

"I need you to take a welcome packet over to our newest client, along with a hearty thank-you from all of us here. So, do you have a pen handy?"

"Uh…yeah, sure. Hang on." Shifting the phone to his left hand, he opened the center armrest and extracted a scrap of paper and a pen from its depths. Then, wedging the phone between his shoulder and his cheek, he propped the paper on his steering wheel and prepared to write. "Okay, shoot."

"Eight-one-six Sunset Street, Winoka."

He repeated it, then capped his pen and popped it back in the armrest compartment. "Got it."

"I know you've been through a lot today, Mark, but as soon as you're able to get this taken care of, the better?"

Oh, how he wanted to say no, to continue on his journey to Bucket List 101 and the conversation he wanted to have with Emily. But tomorrow would be here before he knew it. A new day with the chance for a new start…

"I'll check in on Seth first. If he's still sleeping, I'll deliver."

## Chapter Sixteen

Emily crossed the living room and pulled open the front door, her breath hitching at the sight of Mark standing on the porch, an enormous envelope in his hands. And for a moment, as she drank him in, she allowed herself to remember the way his arms had felt as he'd cradled her after they'd made love—the contentment that had been eluding her for months, if not years, finally hers for the taking.

Yet it had all been a farce.

What had meant so much to her had meant nothing to the man standing on her porch now, looking from her to a scrap of paper in his hand and back again, as if he'd been dropped in the middle of a foreign land.

"What do you want, Mark?" she asked.

"I…" He looked down at the paper one more time and then held it up for her to see. "This is 816 Sunset Street, isn't it?"

And then she knew why he was there. He'd been assigned her case. Though, by the look on his face, she guessed he was still in the dark about that.

"Yes, it is." She knew she was being curt, but couldn't help it. He'd hurt her in a way no one ever had before. And while she understood his stance, it didn't negate the way he'd used her before he dropped the proverbial hammer on her heart and her self-respect.

"I don't understand. I'm virtually certain I jotted down the address exactly as Stan told it to me."

"Considering that's the address I gave him, I'd say you did a good job."

The hand that held her address dropped to his side, and he stared at her, confused. "You talked to Stan? At Folks Helping Folks?"

Met with her silence, he stuffed the paper into his pants pocket and shifted from foot to foot. "Why?"

"Because that's who the receptionist put me through to when I called."

"You called the foundation?"

She shrugged. "How else were they supposed to know I need assistance?"

Mark stepped forward, only to stop when she held up her hands. "Why? Did something happen today after you found Seth? Are you feeling bad?"

It took everything in her power not to turn around and slam the door in his face. This man, who knew nothing about her beyond the lapse of judgment that had allowed her to be a one-night stand, was so quick to assume she was weak. Sickly. And it made her angry.

"For the umpteenth time, Mark, I'm fine. I've been

saddled with a scary-sounding condition, but I'm fine! Not that you'll ever get that or, rather, *want* to get that."

For a moment it was as if she'd slapped him. He drew back, blinked, and then simply looked sad.

She couldn't take it anymore. "Look, I called because I realized I could use my condition to help other people."

At his raised eyebrows, she continued. "By making my business more accessible, with the help of the foundation, I'll be able to provide opportunities to clients I couldn't have otherwise. And if I'm going to hang my hat on being the kind of company that helps people check off items on their bucket lists, I can't ignore the fact that individuals with disabilities and conditions have lists, too."

"So you're going ahead with the assistance just to help others?" he inquired.

Emily hesitated briefly. "At this particular moment in time? Yes. But anything can happen, with me just like with this segment of the population I've been overlooking for far too long. I don't need help now, but I may very well in the future."

"Oh, Emily, I know how hard it must have been to make that call." Mark took another step this time trying to draw her in for a hug. But she stepped back out of his reach.

She didn't need his touch. She didn't need him, period.

"I assume that's the paperwork Stan said he'd send over?" She pointed to the envelope under Mark's arm, and then reached for it at his nod. "I'll look it over, sign what needs to be signed and have Trish bring it by the foundation before week's end. Will that work?"

He relinquished his grasp on the packet and nodded. "Uh...yeah. That should be just fine."

"Well, then, we're done here, yes?" Without waiting for a response, she wrapped her fingers around the edge of the door and tried to push it closed. But when it was just shy of the click, Mark pushed it back open.

"Emily, please. We need to talk about it."

"I'm sure the paperwork is self-explanatory. If I hit a snag, I'll call the office."

He moved his hand from the door to her cheek. "No. We need to talk about what happened the other night. With us."

She covered his hand with hers and closed her eyes for a moment, her heart in a losing battle with her head. "There is no *us,* Mark. Now go home. Be with Seth."

"But—"

Fighting back tears, she kept her voice as steady as possible when she said, "I'd ask you to give him a hug for me and tell him once again how glad I am he's safe and sound, but I also know you don't want me tarnishing his world with my sickly presence."

Again, she tried to close the door. And again, Mark stopped it with his hand.

"Please, Emily. I need to talk to you. For me *and* for Seth."

HE SUPPOSED HE SHOULD look around, maybe comment on the framed photographs or various knickknacks he couldn't quite make out from his spot on her living room sofa, but Mark couldn't.

Not yet, anyway.

All that mattered at that exact moment was finding a way to explain himself and his actions in a way that would wipe the hurt from her big brown eyes once and for all.

"I didn't shut down on you yesterday morning because I didn't care, or because I'd gotten what I wanted and I was done with you." He leaned forward and studied her, her defensive posture alerting him to the battle he had ahead. "Please tell me you know that, Emily. Please."

When she didn't respond, he continued, his desire to cross the space between them and pull her into his arms almost more than he could handle.

*Take it slowly, buddy...*

"You touched something inside me the first moment I laid eyes on you in that orienteering class. It was like someone opened the curtains on my world for the first time in over a year." He saw her swallow, and knew he had her ear, if nothing else. "I guess you could say that part was all physical attraction, and maybe you'd even be right. I mean, look at you! You have the most expressive eyes and breathtaking smile I've ever seen. I'd be a fool if I didn't notice that, Emily. I'd be a fool, too, if I didn't find the way your hair curls around the edges of your face sexy as all get-out. And I'd be a blind fool if I couldn't see how unforgettable your body is."

A hint of red tinged her cheeks and he felt his body react almost instantly. "But it wasn't just a physical reaction. I've seen attractive women before—they're on virtually every corner, if you're of a mind to look. But that initial reaction to you was different, and I'm not sure how, exactly, to explain it beyond that. And then you started talking, and I found myself getting excited about things. *Important* things like life…and living."

"I'm glad my class impacted you like that," she whispered.

He dropped his hands to his thighs and stood up, his attention trained on the woman seated on the other side of the room. "It wasn't the *class* that impacted me like that, Emily. It was you.

"It's one of the reasons I took Seth fishing that night. Because I needed to clear my head. I've only been a widower for six months now, Emily. Six months. What kind of heel can have feelings like that for another woman within six months?"

He was mentally chastising himself for the way his voice was growing raspy when she finally looked up, her eyes fixed on his. "And then there you were…as gorgeous and fun as you'd been in the classroom and in the woods, and you were making my son *smile*."

Running a hand across his mouth, Mark tried to rein in the emotions that threatened to annihilate the courage that had him talking in the first place. "It wasn't an I'll-smile-because-Daddy-just-told-me-a-silly-joke smile or a hooray-we're-having-ice-cream smile, Emily.

It was a real one—the kind I haven't seen on his face in far too long."

"I got as much from Seth as he got from me that night," she finally said. "He made me smile a real smile, too."

"A real smile?" Mark repeated.

She uncrossed her arms and laced her fingers together, twisting them ever so slightly. "Ever since I was diagnosed six months ago, I feel like everyone is always looking at me funny—my mom, Kate, Trish… My clients don't know, of course, but that's a different relationship, anyway. But with Seth, it was like he saw me. The *real* me. The me that even *I* was beginning to doubt was still there."

Mark took a tentative step forward and gestured to the vacant space on the sofa beside Emily. "May I?"

A pause gave way to the faintest of nods.

"It all came crashing down, though, on the way home in the car after pizza. Suddenly that smile on Seth's face was gone, and in its place was worry." Shifting his body, Mark reached for her hand, then stopped, uncertain. "Seth is only four, Emily. *Four*. He's not supposed to worry about anything beyond which kind of milk he wants, chocolate or regular, and which crayon will make his latest castle the most glittery. Yet there he was, sitting in the backseat…worried about you."

"I'm sorry," she murmured.

Pushing aside any residual hesitation, Mark took her hand and squeezed it gently. "No, *I'm* sorry. I'm sorry I didn't call and explain when I decided to bail on the rock climbing because of my own hang-up. But I thought I was doing the right thing. I thought I was protecting my son from another broken heart."

Emily tried to pull her hand away, but Mark held on tight. "That's what I don't get," she stated. "How was rock climbing with me going to break Seth's heart?"

"I saw the worry on his face after spending only two, maybe three hours with you. Can you imagine the concern he'd have for you after really getting to know you?"

At the understanding in her eyes, Mark continued, his voice breaking once again. "I promised Sally I would look after Seth. That I would do everything in my power to keep him happy and safe. And the way I was seeing it at the time, allowing him to get close with someone I knew to be sick would be like purposely ignoring that promise."

"But I'm not going to die from this, Mark. I may not ever show any outward signs that anything's wrong at all."

"I know that now. But even so, there's also a possibility that you could be in a wheelchair in five years. Such a fate for someone as active as you would be awful. Seth is the kind of kid who feels that. Truly feels that."

The slump of her shoulders told Mark she understood.

"But when I saw you again after we didn't show up for the lesson, and we spent all that time together at Kate's, and then later on the climbing walls at your office, it was like I'd forgotten all the reasons I had to stay away from you. And when we made love…in my bed…I was whole again. Until Seth called, anyway. And that's when I remembered that my job, my promise, has me being a father first."

"And so you put up a wall," she mused.

"Yeah, I put up a wall." Taking hold of her other hand, Mark slowly lifted it to his lips and brushed a kiss across her fingertips. "But Seth and Kate made me see that that wall isn't just holding back potential hurt and pain, it's also holding back any chance at true love. For me and for Seth."

Mark watched as Emily closed her eyes and worked to steady her breathing, his own hitching in response when she finally looked at him again through tear-dappled lashes. "True love?" she rasped.

"True love."

# Chapter Seventeen

Emily wanted nothing more than to wrap her arms around Mark and shed the happy tears that were making it difficult to see.

This man loved her. Loved her so much that he was willing to take a chance with his heart and that of his son's.

*On her.*

She'd dreamed of a moment like this for more than half her life. Yet now that it was here, she knew it couldn't be. Not for her, anyway.

To let Mark and his son love her would be unfair.

Slipping her left hand from his, she wiped a finger beneath her eyes, dislodging all tears. "I appreciate what it must have taken for you to come here and say these things to me. And I'm touched. I truly am. But I don't want a relationship, with you or anyone else."

He pulled her hand from her face and held it tightly, scooting closer as he did. "Look, I know I was a jerk, Emily. But I was wrong. I know that."

"Maybe you were, maybe you weren't. But as for you

and me, it's not going to happen." She hated how cruel she sounded, but it needed to be said.

This time, when she pulled her hands away, he let them go, the bewilderment in his face impossible to miss. "Emily. I don't get this. I'm telling you I love you. I want you to be a part of Seth's and my future."

She drew back. "Your future?"

"Of course. What do you think I've been trying to say?"

Silence fell between them as she let his words sink in, their meaning, their sincerity making her wish things were different. That *she* was different. But she wasn't.

She pushed herself off the couch and wandered over to the fireplace, where the countless photographs lined the mantel. There was the picture of her and Kate on a river in Tennessee, the look of horror on her friend's face as they paddled through rapids a stark contrast to the grin on Emily's face. There was the photograph she'd taken while rappelling down a rock wall in Montana. And the gag one Kate had framed of Emily's hair after a week of survival camping in the Colorado Rockies.

Each picture represented a milestone along her path to fulfilling some of her biggest dreams. No, there weren't any wedding poses or cute babies smiling out from any of the frames, but that was okay. In just over thirty years, she'd accomplished more of her dreams than most people did in a lifetime.

"You're in need of a few new pictures, don't you think?"

She spun around to find Mark standing not more than a foot away. "Excuse me?"

"You missed a picture in your office and, because of that, you're missing a few here." He motioned toward the photographs in front of them and smiled. "Fortunately for you, I have one of them with me."

Unsure of what he was talking about, she followed him over to the packet she'd set on the coffee table, and watched as he opened the back flap, withdrawing an all-too-familiar, golden-hued paper.

Emily lifted her hands. "How did you get that?"

Holding the whimsically illustrated page next to his face, he flashed his best knee-weakening smile. "Notice the hair?" He pointed from the prince's head to his own. "Do you see the color?"

"It's Milk Chocolate," she whispered.

"Uh-huh…" He pointed to his own hair once again, before drawing her attention back to the picture. "And the eyes? What were those? Royal something or other?"

She swallowed and shook her head. "Ocean Wave Blue."

"Ocean Wave Blue, eh?" He smirked. "Uh-huh. Got those, too, don't I? And if you use just a little imagination, you'll see that my muscles aren't so far off, either." He hooked an arm upward and flexed his biceps, eliciting a laugh from her.

When her laughter began to fade, he grabbed her

hand once again. "I can be this guy, Emily. I can be your prince. I just happen to have a second, and far cuter, prince in tow. That's the only difference."

Oh, how she wished that were true.

Wriggling her hand free of his, she took the drawing and turned it so he could see the whole picture. "But that's not the only difference, Mark. Not by a long shot."

"Then help me see what I'm missing," he pleaded.

She smacked her free hand against the other figure depicted there. "*She's* different!"

"Not really." He stepped forward and, reaching out, captured a piece of Emily's hair between his fingers. "Same blond locks, just a little shorter." He released it and brushed the back of his hand down the side of her face. "Eyes are just as big and brown as ever. Though you left off one of my favorite parts when you opted not to draw in your freckles."

She closed her eyes against a burning that had nothing to do with happiness and everything to do with the fact that her heart was breaking over the one dream she knew she couldn't have, no matter how desperately she wished otherwise. When she opened them again, she saw the face of a man who'd spent the past thirty minutes being honest about his feelings. The least she could do was do the same.

"I'm not talking about the stuff you can see. I'm talking about the stuff you can't."

"Like what? Because I can't see your spirit in this drawing, but it's plain as the nose on my face. And I can't see inside your heart in this, either, but I saw it when you made Seth feel special on the beach, and at the pizza parlor later that same night. And I *felt* it when we were together at Kate's barbecue, and when we held each other after we'd made love."

"Stop!" she shouted. "I'm not talking about that kind of stuff. I'm talking about being a burden."

He held up his palms. "Whoa, whoa, whoa. A burden? A burden to whom?"

"To you, to Seth, to anyone who signs on to spend their life with me." She allowed herself one more glance at the drawing she'd been so proud of twenty years earlier, and then tossed it into the hearth, to be burned on the first cool night. "I may not die from this disease, but I might very well be in a wheelchair or wasting away on a couch, making you feel as if you can't enjoy your life or Seth's because you're stuck at home taking care of me. And then what kind of life will you have? What kind of life will Seth have?"

"Emily, hold on a minute. Wasn't it you who said you might live out the rest of your days as if nothing was wrong with you?"

"Might is the key word, Mark. *Might*. That's not enough of an assurance for me."

"And if the worst case happens, I'll take care of you. I'll carry you to the car so we can go for a drive. I'll carry you up the side of a mountain so we can have a picnic with a view. I'll carry you to bed so I can make love to you and then hold you all night. And I'll do all of those things because I *want* to."

"Carry me?" she spit. "*Carry* me? Oh, no…" She crossed the living room with quick, even strides and stopped just shy of the front door. "A very wise man recently told me something that will stay with me forever. He said we come into this life alone, and we'll leave it that way, too. So living it that way from point A to point B really isn't such an *awful* thing."

"Awful? Maybe not. But *sad?* You bet it is."

She felt the sting in her eyes and knew it wouldn't be long before tears made it past her lashes. "He's not sad. He's determined. Like me."

"Maybe he is. And if he is, then good for him. But being determined and allowing yourself to love and be loved aren't mutually exclusive things, Emily. Sure, you made all those pictures on your office wall come true on your own. That's awesome. But is there any reason those same dreams couldn't have come true with a supportive partner by your side? I don't think so. And if that supportive partner can step in and make things a little easier along the way, is that so wrong?"

"Maybe I *want* to do it by myself."

"Do you?" Mark pressed. "Do you really? Because I don't think you do—"

She opened the door and stepped to the side to indicate her desire for him to leave. "I won't push this disease off on anyone else. It's mine to live with, not yours."

After several long moments, Mark joined her by

the door, the determination in his eyes taking her breath away. "Love isn't a burden, Emily. It's a journey. Through good times and bad. And I for one would rather have five minutes of wonderful than a lifetime of nothing special."

She brought her hand to her mouth in an effort to stifle the sobs that were building. "I never wanted to be carried through life. I wanted to be the perfect wife, the perfect mother."

"And being in a wheelchair negates that?"

"When your child wants to play with blocks and you have to watch from five feet away, yes. When you want to make your husband his favorite dinner, but can't because the ingredients you need are too high for you to reach from a seated position, yes. When you can't walk your child to the bus stop, hand in hand, on his first day of school, yes."

"Emily, it doesn't have to be like that."

"The fact that it might be is enough for me." She tried to resist when Mark pulled her close, but she couldn't. More than anything she wanted to savor the feel of his arms one more time, to find whatever comfort she could in knowing that her dream could have come true.

All too soon, though, he stepped back, his hand reaching for hers in the process. "Come with me. There's something I want to show you."

HE HELD HER HAND all the way to the front door, a wave of second thoughts accompanying him. While there was a part of him that liked the idea of Seth being present when Mark asked Emily to marry him, there was another part that was just plain scared. Scared she wouldn't see things the way he saw them.

"You can open your eyes now," he prompted. "Just don't look around too much out here, okay?"

"Don't look around too much?"

"Humor me." He wasn't entirely sure she would remember the house, considering the heightened stress level they'd been under when they'd pulled up the driveway the first time. But he didn't want to take any chances. Her focus was needed inside.

"Where are we?" she asked as he gave a quick knock and opened the door for her to enter.

"You'll see." He knew he was being cryptic, but he wanted her to see reality with her own two eyes. With any luck, it would have more impact than any picture he could try to paint with his words.

Step by step, he led her down the main hallway, his slow, careful gait designed to give her time to soak up the various degrees and awards that were displayed on the walls.

"Rose Reynolds?" Emily read as they passed. "Who is that?"

The sound of his son's happy chatter saved Mark from having to verbalize an answer. "Do I hear my little man?" he called.

"I'm in here, Daddy. With Gam."

Emily tugged him to a stop. "You brought me to your

mother's house?" she whispered. "Mark, what on earth are you doing?"

His only response was to guide her the rest of the way down the hall and into the hearth room. When they rounded the corner, he released her hand and stopped beside the card table he'd erected before leaving for Kate's that afternoon. "Mom? I brought someone special I'd like you to meet."

Rose Reynolds craned her neck around in greeting, but it was Seth's voice that dominated the room. "Emily! Emily! You're here!" Jumping down from his chair beside his grandmother, he ran to Emily and wrapped his arms around her legs. "Gam and I are building a castle with my blocks. You wanna see?"

"Uh, sure, sweetheart. I'd love to see it." Without glancing in Mark's direction, Emily followed Seth around the table, stopping beside Mark's mother and extending her hand. "Hi. I'm Emily Todd. I'm a friend of—"

His mom's eyes twinkled in the reflection of the overhead light. "I'm Rose and I know who you are. My grandson has talked nonstop about you since the other night at the beach."

At the first hint of a blush on Emily's face, the woman laughed. "In fact, this room right here—" she pointed toward the elaborate block castle's second story "—is yours."

"Mine?" Emily repeated.

"Yupper doodles," Seth exclaimed. "It's big enough for you *and* Daddy!"

The corner of Rose's mouth twitched just before a sly smile broke out across her gently lined face. "Emily, would you like something to drink? I have wine, lemonade, water, tea…."

At Emily's questioning glance, Mark nodded.

"I'd love a glass of water if it's not too much trouble."

"No trouble at all."

Seth's finger shot up into the air. "I'll be right back, Emily. Don't go anywhere, okay?" Then, in a flash, he was around the table and climbing up onto his grandmother's lap as she wheeled herself from the table and into the kitchen.

Mark watched as his mother transported his son across the kitchen and then went about the task of filling Emily's drink order. After a moment, he looked back at Emily.

"Your mom…she's in a wh-wheelchair," Emily stammered.

"Yup." He pointed toward the card table between them. "Doesn't stop her from building a castle with her grandson, now, does it?"

When Emily said nothing, he nodded toward the kitchen. "And Seth? He's just as happy to ride around the house on his grandmother's lap as he would be to walk by her side. It's his grandma and that's all that matters."

When Emily finally spoke, her voice was quiet and

unsure. "But what about when he gets too big to ride in her lap?"

"He'll push her…just like I did."

Emily's lower lip trembled ever so slightly. "She was in that when you were a kid?"

"She's been in it since *she* was a kid. Mom lost her leg in a fire. She's got an artificial one, but that's mostly for vanity, as she's fond of saying. Which means—" he looked closely at Emily "—she was in it when she married my dad."

Mark watched as Emily peered around the room.

"He's not here anymore, unfortunately."

"Oh? Did he pack up and leave when he realized how much work she was going to be?"

"He died just before Seth was born. Mom cared for him right up until the end."

Emily's face turned crimson. "Mark, I'm sorry. That was out of line."

He shrugged. "I imagine a first glance at the two of them would have had lots of people assuming he cared for her. But by the second glance, anyone with half a brain in their head would realize they were as much a partnership as any other marriage out there. The only difference was the fact that Mom did most everything from a seated position."

"But she has all those awards and degrees," Emily mused.

"You're right, she does." Mark knew it was premature to get his hopes up, but things were looking good.

Emily was getting a taste of a reality she needed to see. "And knowing Mom, she's likely to add a few more to her collection before she gets around to admitting she's old. Heck, she'd probably remarry one day if she could find someone to keep up with her."

Even as he spoke, he could tell Emily wasn't absorbing what he said. Instead, her eyes were focused to the side, as if she was trying to remember something.

"Wait. One of those degrees we passed was for…" Her words trailed off as she headed along the hallway, with Mark on her heels. When she reached the row of framed certificates, she stopped in front of the one that was dead center. Tapping her hand on the glass, she looked from the official document to Mark and back again, the confusion in her face making him chuckle. "This says she's scuba qualified."

"Because she is."

"But how?"

"When she and Dad were in Australia on vacation fifteen years ago, she came across a place that offered scuba classes to people like her."

"But you can't scuba dive in a chair, Mark," Emily protested.

"And she didn't. They removed her artificial leg, attached an extra-big flipper to her good foot and away she went, compliments of—"

"The water's buoyancy," Emily finished. "Wow. I had no idea."

"It's been like that with my mom for as long as I

can remember. Everything she's done in life, everything she's ever accomplished, she's done *in spite* of her chair." Seeing in Emily's eyes the emotion he'd hoped to stimulate, he took her hand and led her back to the living room. Then, with determination, he pulled her close, his shoulder quickly growing damp from her quiet tears. "Which is how I've always loved her. And how Seth has always loved her, too. Why I didn't look at things that way from the start is beyond me, but I guess I just needed to step back and take in the big picture. And you do, too."

"I can't make any promises," Emily whispered.

"Neither can I. Not about that kind of stuff, anyway. But there is one promise I know I can make if you'll let me."

"What's that?" She stepped back and peered up at him.

"Seth? Can you come here a second?" Mark called. "I need your help with something."

"Sure, Daddy." The boy rode across the kitchen on his grandmother's lap, then climbed down carefully with the water glass in his hand. "Here you go, Emily. I hope it's really yummy."

Taking his son by the hand, Mark knelt on the floor at Emily's feet and whispered to Seth to do the same. Then, looking up, he met and held her gaze. "I promise, from this day forward, to sweep you off your feet and carry you in my arms only if you ask. With one caveat, of course."

The smile he'd grown to love in such a short period of time slowly made its way across her face in spite of the tears that streamed down her cheeks. "What's that?" she asked quietly.

"That I don't have to ask permission to carry you over the threshold of our home on our wedding night."

# Epilogue

Trish looked up from her desk the second they walked in, the smile on her face surely a reflection of the one Emily felt spreading across her own.

"Hey, boss. Hey, Seth. Ready for the big day?" Spinning around in her desk chair, Emily's assistant yanked open her top drawer, pulled out a bouquet of lollipops and held it out for Seth to see. "They taste just like vanilla ice cream, only not so cold."

Emily shook her head and laughed, releasing Seth's hand as she did. "Now, wait a minute, Trish. Are you *my* assistant or *Seth's?*"

"I got a cherry one for you, boss."

"Good answer," she joked before reaching for the series of pink sticky notes lined up across the desk. "So everything's all set for noon?"

"Everything is all set. I even gave a call to that reporter from *Winoka Magazine* who did that article on you last spring. Told her what's going on, and she said she'd send a photographer by to snap some pictures of the ribbon cutting for the next issue."

"Outstanding." Emily flipped through the messages that had come into the office while she'd been away for her appointment. When she got to the fourth in the pile, she stole a peek in Trish's direction. "Kate called?"

Pulling an orange lollipop from her mouth, her assistant nodded, her expression giving nothing away where Kate's call was concerned.

"And? What did she say?"

"She's on her way over."

"Did she say why?" Emily prompted.

Trish made a face. "We're talking about Kate, aren't we? Everyone around her is supposed to be an open book. But her? Not unless she's in your face."

"True." Emily smiled at Seth as he hopped across the main office and down the hall, a lollipop held tightly in his hand.

Trish watched him go and then turned back with a questioning look. "Have I missed the memo about our little prince turning into a frog? Because if I did, might I remind you it usually happens the other way around. You know, first the frog, then the prince."

Glancing at the note containing nothing but Kate's name, Emily shrugged. "He's still a prince. He's just a prince who's learning about the letter *B* in his kindergarten class this week. Bunnies start with *B,* so there's going to be a lot of hopping going on."

"Ah-h-h… I see." Trish lowered her voice. "Everything go okay with your neurologist this morning?"

"Nothing I didn't anticipate."

At the sudden shift in her tone, Trish's eyebrow shot upward once again. "You okay?"

"Yeah, I'm okay. Just found myself marveling once again at the psychic ability I appeared to have had when I was ten."

When she didn't elaborate, Trish waved her down the hall. "And apparently you and Kate both excelled in whatever class you guys took on the art of being cryptic."

Emily made a face at her young friend before heading off to her office. She wasn't trying to be cryptic. It just didn't make much sense to talk about something that simply wasn't going to happen. It was like strapping on her climbing gear, only to find herself standing in the middle of a flat desert. There was no point. Not in her eyes, anyway.

Besides, if she shared the reason for her appointment aloud, it would seem as if she wasn't happy with the life she had, and that couldn't be further from the truth. She already had so much more than she'd thought she'd ever have.

"Hiya, Memmy."

She couldn't help but smile at the nickname the little boy had bestowed on her after the wedding, his creative merging of her name with the role she'd be playing in his life resulting in a moniker they both treasured.

"Your *bunny* hop was very good, sweetheart."

Seth beamed around his lollipop. "Really?"

She crossed the room to perch on the edge of her desk. "Actually, I'd say it was *beautiful, brave* and very *believable.*"

His closed his lips around the sucker for a quick taste and then popped it out of his mouth. "That's very good, Memmy. Miss Olson would be proud of how well you know your *B*s."

"I'm pretty proud of Memmy, too. But for lots of other reasons, little man."

Hearing her husband's voice coming down the hall, Emily turned toward the door, the sight of her real live prince making all her petty worries disappear. This man, whom she adored with everything she had, had given her back her dream. Life didn't get much better, in her opinion.

He opened his arms wide enough for both of them, his first kiss finding the top of Seth's head and the second one lingering on Emily's lips. "How'd it go today?" he whispered in her ear.

"I asked those last few questions we discussed, and I think it's best if we just stay the course."

When Seth wiggled free and returned to the reading corner Emily had set up for him behind her desk, she allowed Mark to pull her close, the comfort she found in his arms making her decision a little easier.

"You know I'll support whatever you decide."

She gestured over her shoulder at the fifth drawing,

now framed and hung on the wall beside all the others, and lowered her voice to a near whisper. "I drew all of those because they represented my fondest dreams. And one by one, they've all come true. There are no other drawings to be framed, because I already have everything I ever wanted, Mark. To risk jeopardizing my ability to care for Seth just so I can complete a picture I never drew in the first place just isn't worth it to me."

"I love you, Emily."

"I love—"

The buzz of the intercom cut her off midsentence. "Boss? Are you ready?"

She glanced from the clock over the door to Mark and then Seth's face. All her life she'd been a go-getter, determined to make her dreams and the dreams of everyone around her come true. Nineteen months ago, an obstacle had been erected in her quest to reach her greatest dream of all. Thirteen months ago, Mark and Seth had stood beside her as she made the choice to see that obstacle as an opportunity to grow.

Now it was her turn to do the same for a man she'd only met over the phone.

"We're ready." Holding her hands out to her two greatest gifts, Emily made her way back down the hallway with her big prince on one side and her little prince on the other. When she reached the end, she turned right instead of left, bypassing the front door in favor of the new, wider one that had been installed by the Folks Helping Folks Foundation.

Pushing it open, she closed her eyes and lifted her face to the late August sun. "Mmm…"

"Mrs. Reynolds?"

Her lashes parted to reveal the man who, in many ways, was responsible for leading her back to Mark. A man who knew what it was to dream, and embodied the very spirit needed to make those dreams come true. She started to walk down the ramp to shake his hand, but stopped when he shook his head and wheeled himself up to her instead, the smile on his rugged face making her blink back tears.

"Mr. Walker, I am honored to finally meet you. Our time on the phone together so many months ago made such a difference in my life. All I can do now is hope that what we've added here today will make a difference in yours, too."

"It's a start, that's for sure. At least now I can come here and learn about some of the things I put off doing until I wasn't able to do them anymore."

Emily glanced up at Mark, saw him nod, and knew the moment she'd been researching and working toward was finally here. At least the first part, anyway.

Pointing toward the door she'd just come through, she addressed Mr. Walker with what she hoped was a semidecent poker face. "Before we get started with the foundation's ribbon-cutting ceremony, would you mind coming inside with me for a second? I'd like to show you something."

"Sure." Jed rested his hands on the wheels of his

chair and spun them forward, through the door Mark held open. Room by room, Emily guided him through the building, pausing to explain about the various on-site classes they held throughout the year, as well as a few details about the adventures that took them to various locations throughout Winoka and beyond.

When they reached the last classroom before the hallway that led to her office, she stepped inside and took a seat, gesturing for him to follow in his chair. "Mr. Walker, you already know it was that initial phone call you made to Trish last year that set the ball rolling to get our doors widened and that ramp put in place. And for that, we're grateful. You see, I'm a big believer in helping people realize their dreams, and making our building accessible got us a little closer to doing that."

At Jed's nod, she continued, motioning for a teary-eyed Trish in the doorway to join them for the rest of the surprise. "Anyway, I know you'd like to be able to do more than just wheel your way through a door and sit in on a few classes. And you should be able to, as should anyone else who's confined to a wheelchair. So I sent out a call a few months ago to find an adventure instructor who is familiar with physical challenges."

Jed's mouth gaped ever so slightly as he looked from Emily to Trish and back again. "And?"

"When the ribbon-cutting ceremony is done, I'd like to introduce you to Peter Cummings. He's a dynamite kid with some really great ideas and the know-how to implement them."

Her eyes began to burn at Jed's obvious struggle for words. Unable to contain herself anymore, she took both his hands in hers and smiled. "And as for you, Mr. Walker? You're the first name on my list for a scuba trip to Saint John this winter."

"Scuba?" he repeated in a voice thick with emotion.

"That's right. *Scuba.*" She looked toward the door once again and cleared her throat. Less than thirty seconds later, she was reengaging eye contact with Jed as Mark piloted Rose into the room. "And my mother-in-law, right here, will be on that trip, too. Seems the first five times she went diving weren't enough."

Jed's hands trembled in Emily's, though his focus was on no one but Rose. "You've done it? You've been under the ocean like that?"

The older woman's smile lit up the room. "You bet I have. And in a few months, you'll be able to say the very same thing."

Grateful and deeply moved, Emily released one of Jed's hands in order to grab one of Rose's. "Jed, you made me realize my vision for Bucket List 101 was lacking in one very important way. The changes you see here today have hopefully altered that. But I've learned something else, too. I've learned that doing things on my own is very different than doing them alone. And while you may have been right on the phone all those months ago when you reminded me that I came into this world alone and will leave it the same way, I have to tell you that all the time in between is so much better when you have someone you love and respect by your side. The key is finding someone who really sees you, regardless of whether you're sitting, standing or somewhere in between."

SHE WAS ROUNDING UP the last of the paper plates when Kate came bursting through the door with her four-month-old daughter, Lizzie, fast asleep in her carrier. "Oh, thank God. I was hoping the two of you would still be here."

Mark popped his head up from the corner where he was dismantling the PA system they'd rented for the ribbon-cutting ceremony, and laughed. "Was that your car that just came screeching into the parking lot a second ago?"

"Nope. That was Miss Trish heading out. Which works perfectly, since I need to talk to the two of you alone." Kate scanned the room and then poked her head into the hall. "Where's Seth?"

"He's in my office drawing a picture." Emily dumped the stack of dirty plates into the trash and made a bee-line for Lizzie. "Am I ever going to get to see her when she's awake?"

"Come by around dinner or anytime during the night and you'll see her wide-eyed and bushy-tailed." At Mark's snicker, Kate rolled her eyes. "You think I'm kidding?"

"No. Actually, I don't. Seth was like that, too, when he was that age."

Emily ran a gentle hand down her goddaughter's leg as Mark and Kate swapped the kind of stories she'd never experienced. Not firsthand, anyway. And knowing what she now knew about the risk to her health if she became pregnant, they weren't the kind of stories she'd ever be able to relate to. But that was okay. She'd come into Seth's life at such an early age that she hadn't missed too much.

"Woo hoo? Earth to Emily! Come in, Emily."

At the sound of her name, she looked up to find both Mark and Kate gazing at her curiously. "I'm sorry, I guess I zoned out there for a minute."

Mark pulled up a chair next to her and draped his arm over her shoulders. "That's okay, Em. You've more than earned yourself a little zone-out."

Kate sat on the table next to Lizzie's carrier and got straight to the point. "So, have you made a decision?"

From anyone else, the question would have been too much. But from Kate, it was okay. Normal, even. Taking a deep breath, Emily willed herself to choose her words wisely.

"Having MS doesn't mean I can't have a child. We can. But in order to try, I'd have to stop my injections. If it worked, and we became pregnant, I'd have to stay off them throughout the duration of the pregnancy. Lots of women with my condition do it all the time. But a large percentage of them experience an acceleration of the disease within six months of giving birth."

Mark whispered a kiss across the side of her head as

she continued. "If we didn't already have Seth, I might be tempted to take the chance. But we do. And I want to be healthy for him and for Mark for as long as possible."

Kate covered her eyes with her palms.

"Kate? Are you okay?" Mark asked.

Slowly, she pulled her hands from her face and nodded. "I'm better than okay. In fact, I think I have some news that'll blow your minds."

"Okay, shoot."

"Joe's cousin called the other day. The two of you met him at one of our barbecues last spring. His eighteen-year-old daughter is pregnant, and she's going to be giving her baby up for adoption as soon as it's born."

"That's too bad," Mark murmured, tightening his hold on Emily.

"Well, it is and it isn't. You see, Reagan doesn't want to be a mom right now. She's one of those kids who has a life plan, and having a baby doesn't figure on the list right now. She wants to go to college and travel before she even considers settling down and starting a family. The father has relinquished his rights already, and Reagan is ready to do the same, provided she can find a loving family for her little girl."

Mark sat up tall. "Little girl?"

Kate grinned. "Yup. You interested?"

Emily turned to Mark, their simultaneous "yes" eliciting a squeal from Kate and summoning Seth from the hallway.

"Seth, is that you?" Mark called, buying Emily time to wipe the tears from her cheeks.

"Yupper doodle. I have a picture for you and Memmy."

"Hi, Seth!" Kate said. "Come and say hi to Lizzie. Daddy and Memmy woke her up."

Seth hopped over to the baby, who rewarded his efforts with a smile. Smiling back at her, he held his picture up in front of his face and then peeked back and forth between Lizzie and his drawing.

"Can I see your picture, Seth?" Kate asked.

"Sure!'

Kate's eyes widened as she took the golden-hued paper from his hands. "Em? Mark? Uh, you might want to check this out."

Together, they stood and came around the table, their son's latest artistic efforts making everyone gasp.

There, on the paper, was Seth's version of Emily and her prince. Only in his drawing, there were two additional faces.

The first, a little boy, looked just like Seth. Right down to the Sunshine Yellow hair and the same eye color as the prince. In his arms was a baby girl with Strawberry Banana hair and Emerald Green eyes....

Emily turned to Mark, unable to form the question he was able to ask.

"What is this, little man?"

"It's the next picture for Memmy's wall."

* * * * *

## COMING NEXT MONTH
### from Harlequin® American Romance®

AVAILABLE OCTOBER 30, 2012

## #1425 BEAU: COWBOY PROTECTOR
*Harts of the Rodeo*
### Marin Thomas

Nothing scares bull rider Beau Adams—except the thought of losing Sierra Byrnes. But how can she commit to Beau when impending blindness makes her own future so uncertain?

## #1426 A FOREVER CHRISTMAS
*Forever, Texas*
### Marie Ferrarella

Deputy Sheriff Gabriel Rodriguez saves the life of a mysterious woman and introduces his "Angel" to the cozy small town. Will her true identity destroy their blossoming romance?

## #1427 CHRISTMAS IN TEXAS
### Tina Leonard and Rebecca Winters

A special treat for American Romance readers this Christmas— 2 stories featuring rugged Texan heroes by 2 of your favorite authors!

## #1428 THE TEXAS RANCHER'S MARRIAGE
*Legends of Laramie County*
### Cathy Gillen Thacker

Chase Armstrong and Merri Duncan decide to provide a home for orphaned twins, and have another baby, all with no expectation of romantic love. So why is life suddenly getting so complicated?

# REQUEST YOUR FREE BOOKS!
## 2 FREE NOVELS PLUS 2 FREE GIFTS!

## Harlequin®

### American ★ Romance®

## LOVE, HOME & HAPPINESS

**YES!** Please send me 2 FREE Harlequin® American Romance® novels and my 2 FREE gifts (gifts are worth about $10). After receiving them, if I don't wish to receive any more books, I can return the shipping statement marked "cancel." If I don't cancel, I will receive 4 brand-new novels every month and be billed just $4.49 per book in the U.S. or $5.24 per book in Canada. That's a saving of at least 14% off the cover price! It's quite a bargain! Shipping and handling is just 50¢ per book in the U.S. and 75¢ per book in Canada.* I understand that accepting the 2 free books and gifts places me under no obligation to buy anything. I can always return a shipment and cancel at any time. Even if I never buy another book, the two free books and gifts are mine to keep forever.

154/354 HDN FEP2

| Name | (PLEASE PRINT) | |
|------|----------------|---|
| Address | | Apt. # |
| City | State/Prov. | Zip/Postal Code |

Signature (if under 18, a parent or guardian must sign)

### Mail to the **Reader Service:**
**IN U.S.A.:** P.O. Box 1867, Buffalo, NY 14240-1867
**IN CANADA:** P.O. Box 609, Fort Erie, Ontario L2A 5X3

Not valid for current subscribers to Harlequin American Romance books.

**Want to try two free books from another line?**
**Call 1-800-873-8635 or visit www.ReaderService.com.**

* Terms and prices subject to change without notice. Prices do not include applicable taxes. Sales tax applicable in N.Y. Canadian residents will be charged applicable taxes. Offer not valid in Quebec. This offer is limited to one order per household. All orders subject to credit approval. Credit or debit balances in a customer's account(s) may be offset by any other outstanding balance owed by or to the customer. Please allow 4 to 6 weeks for delivery. Offer available while quantities last.

**Your Privacy**—The Reader Service is committed to protecting your privacy. Our Privacy Policy is available online at www.ReaderService.com or upon request from the Reader Service.

We make a portion of our mailing list available to reputable third parties that offer products we believe may interest you. If you prefer that we not exchange your name with third parties, or if you wish to clarify or modify your communication preferences, please visit us at www.ReaderService.com/consumerchoice or write to us at Reader Service Preference Service, P.O. Box 9062, Buffalo, NY 14269. Include your complete name and address.

HAR11B

Discover the magic of Christmas with two
holiday stories of love and forgiveness in

# CHRISTMAS IN TEXAS

## *Christmas Baby Blessings*

### by TINA LEONARD

Capri Snow isn't happy when she discovers
that the Bridesmaids Creek Christmastown Santa is her
almost-ex-husband and cop, Seagal West. But when danger
strikes, Seagal steps in to protect his wife, no matter the cost.

### &

## *The Christmas Rescue*

### by REBECCA WINTERS

When Texas Ranger Flynn Patterson saves Andrea Sinclair
and her infant child from her stalker ex-husband, he finds
himself in more danger than just losing his heart.

**Bring the magic of Christmas home
this November 2012.**

**Available wherever books are sold.**

*When Forever, Texas's newest deputy, Gabe Rodriguez,
rescues a woman from the scene of an accident, he
encounters a mystery, as well.*

*Here's a sneak peek at A FOREVER CHRISTMAS
by* USA TODAY *bestselling author Marie Ferrarella,
available November 2012
from Harlequin® American Romance®.*

It was still raining. Not nearly as bad as it had been earlier,
but enough to put out what there still was of the fire. Mick
was busy hooking up his tow truck to what was left of the
woman's charred sedan and Alma was getting back into her
Jeep. Neither one of them saw the woman in Gabe's truck
suddenly sit up as he started the vehicle.

"No!"

The single word tore from her lips. There was terror in
her eyes, and she gave every indication that she was going
to jump out of the truck's cab—or at least try to. Surprised,
Gabe quickly grabbed her by the arm with his free hand.

"I wouldn't recommend that," he told her.

The fear in her eyes remained. If anything, it grew even
greater.

"Who are you?" the blonde cried breathlessly. She appeared completely disoriented.

"Gabriel Rodriguez. I'm the guy who pulled you out of
your car and kept you from becoming a piece of charcoal."

Her expression didn't change. It was as if his words
weren't even registering. Nonetheless, Gabe paused, giving
her a minute as he waited for her response.

But the woman said nothing.

"Okay," he coaxed as he drove toward the town of
Forever, "your turn."

The world, both inside the moving vehicle and outside of it, was spinning faster and faster, making it impossible for her to focus on anything. Moreover, she couldn't seem to pull her thoughts together. Couldn't get past the heavy hand of fear that was all but smothering her.

"My turn?" she echoed. What did that mean, her turn? Her turn to do what?

"Yes, your turn," he repeated. "I told you my name. Now you tell me yours."

Her name.

The two words echoed in her brain, encountering only emptiness. Suddenly very weary, she strained hard, searching, waiting for something to come to her.

But nothing did.

The silence stretched out. Finally, just before he repeated his question again, she said in a small voice, hardly above a whisper, "I can't."

*Who is this mystery woman?*
*Find out in A FOREVER CHRISTMAS*
*by Marie Ferrarella, coming November 2012*
*from Harlequin® American Romance®.*

# Kathryn Springer

**inspires with her tale of a soldier's promise
and his chance for love in**

# The Soldier's Newfound Family

When he returns to Texas from overseas, U.S. Marine
Carter Wallace makes good on a promise: to tell a fallen
soldier's wife that her husband loved her. But widowed
Savannah Blackmore, pregnant and alone, shares a different
story with Carter—one that tests everything he believes.
Now the marine who never needed anyone suddenly
needs Savannah. Will opening his heart be the
bravest thing he'll ever do?

## ►TEXAS TWINS◄

*Available November 2012*

www.LoveInspiredBooks.com

LI87776

Find yourself
**BANISHED TO THE HAREM**
in a glamorous and tantalizing new tale from

# *Carol Marinelli*

Playboy Sheikh Prince Rakhal Alzirz has time for
one more fling in London before he must return
to his desert kingdom—and Natasha Winters has
caught his eye. He seizes the chance to discover if
Natasha is as fiery in bed as her flaming red hair,
but their recklessness has consequences.... She
might be carrying the Alzirz heir!

# BANISHED
# TO THE HAREM

**Available October 16!**

www.Harlequin.com

HPI3103